Gone

The Missing Years of Bjorn Esterday

Book 26

Conversation Station

2030-2035

Lesson Plans for Groups or Individuals

Wynter Sommers

Wynter Sommers

This work is registered with the UK Copyright Service, in accordance with the Copyright, Designs and Patents Act 1988
All rights reserved 284718038 for

GONE: The Missing Years of Bjorn Esterday

USA Copyright © 2015 GJ dePillis
© TXu002023789 and TXu002010532 / 2016

Library of Congress Control Number: **2021936597**

Published by Pure Force Enterprises, Inc.
California, USA
Since 2002

INGRAM
INGRAM® Distribution

All rights reserved. All rights reserved. No part of this book may be used or reproduced by any means, graphic, electronic, or mechanical, including photocopying, recording, taping or by any information storage retrieval system without the written permission of the authors except in the case of brief quotations embodied in critical articles and reviews.
This novel is a work of fiction. Names, places, characters, and incidents are either the product of the author's imagination or, if real, are used fictitiously.
ISBN-13: 978-1-7184-0053-5 I
ISBN-101-7184-0053-5
GONE BUNDLE SET (26 BOOKS) 978-1-7184-0056-6

DEDICATION

To those who feel strongly about truth, justice, and the integrity of America; your honorable actions make us proud.

To those who wonder if their daily choices matter; your small decisions impact generations to come.

To those everyday people who don't think they have what it takes; your perseverance and strive for the extraordinary, makes the impossible a reality.

To those who have failed; know you will make it and tomorrow will be better.

Your dreams today become our future tomorrow.
Thank you for everything you do.

Wynter Sommers

Bjorn Esterday Was Not Born Yesterday Series

Firebrand (15 Volumes+Conversation Station Book)
Edges (9 Stories +Conversation Station Book)
Gone (24 Stories + Conversation Station Book + Longfellow Journal for 26 books in Gone set)

Bjorn EDGES Series
EDGES Book 1-Swift Encounter
EDGES Book 2-Rousing Attack
EDGES Book 3-One Foot Under
EDGES Book 4-Earthshake
EDGES Book 5-Broken String
EDGES Book 6-Key Witness
EDGES Book 7-Who is She?
EDGES Book 8-Vanish
EDGES Book 9-Chase or Die

Bjorn Series Alternate Reading Plan

1st	Edges Book 1	25th	Gone Book 11
2nd	Edges Book 2	26th	Firebrand Vol 10
3rd	Gone Book 1	27th	Gone Book 12
4th	Firebrand Vol 1	28th	Gone Book 13
5th	Edges Book 3	29th	Firebrand Vol 11
6th	Firebrand Vol 2	30th	Gone Book 14
7th	Gone Book 2	31st	Gone Book 15
8th	Gone Book 3	32nd	Firebrand Vol 12
9th	Firebrand Vol 3	33rd	Gone Book 16
10th	Gone Book 4	34th	Gone Book 17
11th	Firebrand Vol 4	35th	Firebrand Vol 13
12th	Gone Book 5	36th	Gone Book 18
13th	Gone Book 6	37th	Gone Book 19
14th	Gone Book 25-*Longfellow's Journal*	38th	Edges Book 5
		39th	Edges Book 6
15th	Edges Book 4	40th	Gone Book 20
16th	Firebrand Vol 5	41st	Gone Book 21
17th	Gone Book 7	42nd	Edges Book 7
18th	Firebrand Vol 6	43rd	Gone Book 22
19th	Gone Book 8	44th	Firebrand Vol 14
20th	Firebrand Vol 7	45th	Firebrand Vol 15 (End)
21st	Gone Book 9	46th	Edges Book 8
22nd	Firebrand Vol 8	47th	Edges Book 9 (End)
23rd	Gone Book 10	48th	Gone Book 23
24th	Firebrand Vol 9	49th	Gone Book 24 (End)

ACKNOWLEDGMENTS

We acknowledge those who actively build peace. We acknowledge all the selfless talent which contributed to creating meaningful tokens of consideration and sharing. We acknowledge that every person has a daily choice of right or wrong... and we thank you for choosing the right, good, honorable path filled with integrity because that is the difficult and brave path. Small choices today become lasting monuments of loving hope tomorrow.

HOW TO INTERPRET THE CHAPTER TITLES

How to read books in the GONE series: Each title has two numbers. The number on the left is the chapter order in this book. The number on the right of "chapter" is the consecutive continuous chapter in the entire series. The number in parentheses is the year and the rest is a chapter title, sometimes sharing which location the chapter takes place.

For example, below is a chapter which appears in GONE Book #03. It is chapter 6, but GONE continuous saga chapter 13. The action takes place in the year 2030 in the location of Brio in the Gardens. The year is in parenthesis.

6 CHAPTER 13: (2030) BRIO: GARDENS

In this book, each Gone series book title is the chapter in this Lesson Plan guide.

CONTENTS

0 CHAPTER How To Use This Book 1

1 Book: Bubble 2030 9

2 Book: AromaX 2030 15

3 Book: Brio 2030 22

4 Book: Courtroom 2031 27

5 Book: Chaos 2030 to 2031 31

6 Book: Dolphin Express 2031 37

7 Book: Rough-N-Ready 2031 42

8 Book: Lab 2031 to 2032 47

9 Book: Strawberry EarthShake 2032-2033 54

10 Book: Narci 2033 59

11 Book: Lock 2033 to 2034 66

12 Book: Village 2033 to 2034 71

13 Book: Cologne 2034 75

14 Book: Dress for the Ball 2034 79

15 Book: Mountain Mansion 2034 84

16 Book: Investigate 2034 89

17 Book: Stasis 2034 95

18 Book: Realize 2034 101

19 Book: Impact 2034 112

20 Book: Key Tracks 2034 118

21 Book: Hub 2031 130

22 Book: Camp 2034 138

23 Book: Plan 2034 144

24 Book: Finally 2035 155

25 Book: Longfellow's Journal   2028 to 2031 164

26 Characters 173

   Meet the Mattick Family. 185

   Meaning of the Mattick Names 189

27 Locations 191

28 Vocabulary (Alphabetized) 197

29 ISBN for all Books 264

30 About The Back Cover Image 269

31 ABOUT Wynter Sommers 292

0 CHAPTER How To Use This Book

This book of conversation station activities (or lesson plans) is intended to spark group conversation, hence the title "conversation station".

Each of the 15 Firebrand volumes address many topics, yet a single theme shall be highlighted in this Conversation Station. Additional discussion topics of interest are addressed in the "Did You Know" section, which is located at the end of each individual volume.

If you do not have a group, it is a great way to ignite a conversation with somebody else who has not been introduced to the series. These activities revolve around a core love of American History , adventure, and fondness for noble and chivalrous gallantry. .

There is one chapter dedicated to each of the volumes. You may consult the appropriate chapter in this book during and after your reading of one of the volumes. This book is intended to highlight an appreciation for Colonial American history as well as hone soft skills in the participants.

Understanding the motives of those in the 1700's and what drove them to fight for freedom is just as important a perspective to understand as is critical thinking to analyze character motives and how those lessons of yesteryear may still apply in modern times. Additionally, group conversation and empathy are valuable skills to develop.

Each volume contains a "vocabulary" section. Those have been collected and alphabetized in this Conversation Station.

Each chapter dedicated to a specific volume in Firebrand contains the following sections:

These sessions are structured to last approximately **60 minutes or more** depending on what you include in your group session. You can have simply a group discussion, in which case the session would be 20 minutes. These sessions are flexible and are to be designed by the group leader.

1) <u>Assignments</u>: Review after class assignments from the previous meeting. This could take longer if you ask the group participants to summarize to the group what they discovered. At the end of the volume review is when the group leader can explain what the assignment is. So in the start of the session, review the previous volume assignment and at the end of the same session, provide details of a new assignment.
    ✓ Estimated Time: **5 minutes**

2) <u>Theme:</u> This is a short theme which is highlighted in this specific book in the series. This is the open topic the group leader may use to start a group conversation. The activities support the theme.
   ✓ Estimated time: **5 minutes**

3) <u>Chapters referenced</u>: This is a list of the chapter titles in the book in the series which has been (or is being) read. The descriptive titles will inform the group leader about outline of events which transpired in the story.
   ✓ Estimated time: **3 minutes**

4) <u>Structured Activities</u>: These are suggestions for group activities. Structured activities may require some leader advance preparation.
   ✓ Estimated time: **24 minutes** (about 12 minutes per activity)

5) <u>Objective Achieved</u>: This summarizes what the participants should get out of this session. State the objective after the structured activities have completed. Ask the group if they think they have achieved this objective with the activities, conversation, introspective analysis, or other elements the group leader may add to this lesson plan. Remember to announce you will start the group discussion and remind the participants of respectful interaction using the suggested RESORTS rules of conversation later in this section.
   ✓ Estimated time: **3 minutes**

6) <u>Group Conversation</u>: These are open ended questions which spark conversation and dialogue in a group setting.
   ✓ Estimated time: **20 minutes** (Depends on how actively loquacious the group may be)

7) <u>Assignments</u> (Optional): Suggested homework to be done solo or in a team. This new assignment is clarified right before this active session ends.
   ✓ Estimated time: **VARIED**. This takes place after the group has been dismissed and is optional. The amount of time it takes to complete this assignment will vary depending on if this is done solo or in a team setting. It also depends on how the group leader defines the output. For example, if it is to do research to have a conversation at the next meeting, the activity will take less time than if the group leader asks for a formally written paper with illustrations.

If you, as the group leader, plan to have a group discussion, there should be some ground rules.

Group Discussion RESORTS Rules:

RESORTS is an anagram to help you remember that the group should conduct conversations with: *Respect, Empathy, Sources, Opportunity, Rebuttal, Timing, Speculation.*

1) **RESPECT**: Profanity, vulgar comments, personal insults, patronizing attitudes, and lewd innuendo is NOT allowed. A dismissive attitude because a person may belong to some group you do not relate to is also frowned upon. The goal is to have a healthy active discussion and allow both friendly and shy participants the opportunity to freely share their ideas.

2) **EMPATHY**: Imagine yourself in the social class or profession of another...would that perspective change your opinion on a certain topic or themed discussion? Avoid blaming others for the opinions they hold.

3) **SOURCES**: If your comment is based on fact, please state the source. For example, "According to the book written by ____, I think the story really should have been this way___" If your comment is based on your personal opinion, please preface that by saying, "I think, in my own opinion, that the character should have chosen a different option instead of the one they took because..."

4) **OPPORTUNITY**: Every person participating has the right and will have the opportunity to speak. If the group is in person, there should be an indicator to state they wish to speak, such as raising a hand. If the group is virtual, then there should be a way to indicate they wish to contribute a thought, such as typing a note to the host they want to say something so the host can take them off mute, or they themselves un-mute their microphone, or indicate with another icon or graphic that you wish to contribute and wait for the host to call the name of that participant. Whatever the mode of telling the group leader they wish to speak, that rule should be set before the discussion begins.

5) **REBUTTAL**: If you are responding to the comment of another person in your group, please clarify that you have a different perspective to share which may contradict or offer a different nuance to the topic or concept shared. It is strongly discouraged to state you disagree and state the name of the person who just spoke. You should disagree with the concept not the person who just shared the idea with which you disagree.

6) **TIMING**: Each comment will be timed. Opinions on the comment just stated shall also be timed and the

speaker will need to stop sharing when the moderator or group leader informs them when their time has run out. The host or group leader should clearly state, "Thank you, [Name], please feel free to share your comment, you have two uninterrupted minutes." This will provide a fair framework for all participants who wish to speak. It also gives the host the right to interrupt after two minutes to give another participant the opportunity to contribute. The host should watch the clock and make sure the conversation does not go on too long.

7) **SPECULATION**: Speculation is permitted to anticipate what you think could happen to a certain character. This speculation may take you outside of the printed story line. Please try to confine your thoughts to be within the world of GONE or EDGES or other Bjorn Esterday books, in the decade of 2030's. Given this book references characters from FIREBRAND, it is acceptable to reference events in the d 1770's.

For example, introducing a space-ship alien attack may be considered "creative", but perhaps not a conversation trajectory everybody in the group could comment on since none of these story lines address life in outer space. It is requested, therefore, that you confine your character and plot speculations to still be within the appropriate time frame and world presented in this series. It is possible to speculate on how the choices of ancestors may impact future generations.

The goal is to encourage conversation and creative thought, but discouraged sparking conflict, resentment, and injured feelings within your group conversation as this will preventing a productive conversation analysis session and it may damage a trust bond which will be build with the group members with each subsequent interaction. The host should provide a safe environment for all participants.

Preparation for Group Structured Activities

Each of these sections will require the group leader to have a physical or virtual place to write or display something so audience can view the group notes.

This structure is a proposed cadence for conducting a formal and repeatable session where the group host or instructor will interact with and keep the group on track and usher them from one section to the next with a specific output obtained by the end of the session.

Group Conversation

This is the proposed method for guiding a group in an open ended discussion of a topic chosen by the group. It could be different each time as the discussion may take various directions. The group host responsibility is to remind the group when the time is coming to a close and thank them for the group participation.

This is a set of questions you can either ponder yourself or you can ask a group to encourage multi participant conversation. The trajectory of the conversation can take you in almost any direction. As the moderator or group leader, you are to be prepared to remind the group that discussion should be respectful, fact-based, or if based on the speaker's opinion, is stated as such in advance or before sharing their ideas in this public forum.

In this forum you can analyze character motivations and speculate about what might happen to the character even beyond the storyline stated in these books. To ensure that no one speaker monopolizes the conversation, you may want to limit each comment to a specified duration of time, such as three to five minutes, and then allow other group members to respond.

Thank the group for their participation and offer them the option to do an optional assignment activity after the group is dismissed.

1 Book: Bubble 2030

Theme

Misinterpretation.

Do your actions make people assume a pattern of behavior about you? What do you do if people have an images of you which is wrong?

Do you feel as if you are alone inside a bubble and cannot change the minds of those who view you as if you are a caged animal of curiosity?

In this story, Bjorn had a reputation for cavalier abandonment. When he vanished, his boss, Sammy Scribe, did not assume Bjorn was in trouble, but that he was irresponsible.

What do your actions say about you?

Chapters Referenced

Book 01	1 CHAPTER 01: (2030) BRIO: COURTROOM: BJORN DREAMING
Bubble	2 CHAPTER 02: (2030) Cell, Sweet Cell
Year 2030	3 CHAPTER 03: (2030) COURTLY CITY: SAMMY'S DAILY MEMO OFFICE: MARIA CARINA –FIND'S BJORN'S REDMAILED WATSON ARTICLE. VIRGINIA HAMM GETS BJORN FIRED

Preparation for Group Structured Activities

Group leader will need: A virtual or physical place to write so audience can see the group notes. A way to interact with the audience. These activities can be assigned as homework or performed with an interactive group.

Structured Activity 1

In a group of people, what are the clues which can tell you that people are lying about a topic.

For example: The whole group has said they have not gone to the beach. Yet three of them have fresh tans or sunburns, sand in their clothes, are wet and one has seaweed around his ankle. Are they lying? Yes.

Identify a group of people who say one thing yet physical evidence contradicts their story. Log the answers to the questions to see if somebody is lying.

1. What neutral question can you ask to evaluate their answer? You should have a "baseline" of how they behave when they are not lying to see if their

reactions differ.

2. What physical evidence contradicts that answer?

3. Ask them something that is unexpected. If they have planned to lie to you, they may have practiced an answer for an anticipated question. If you ask a random unexpected question, you can observe how they react. Liars may stumble.

4. What body language betrays they are nervous or trying to hide information? Are they blushing? Are their nostrils flaring? Are they coughing or clearing their throat? Are they sweating? Are they blinking rapidly? Are they biting their lip or trying to hide their mouth?

5. Listen to their tone of voice. Has it changed?

6. Ask them a questions where the answer will be "no". Observe their manner. Do they look furtively in a different direction? Close their eyes? Stretch out the "no" word for many seconds? Is there hesitation, then an answer? Are they singing it to appear casual?

7. Are they talking more than a reasonable answer would elicit? They may be trying to fill the void with words so you lose track about what they are saying and just move on.

8. Who are they talking about? Is it themselves or are they trying to divert your focus onto another person or issue?

Structured Activity 2

Document how you would repair a damaged reputation.

1. Understand people are slow to change their minds about you. Be patient. They may not forget the malicious gossip spread about you.

2. Pause your usual pattern of communication to give others around you time to heal.

3. Be the first to bring up the topic of the incorrect story about you. Be concise, factual, brief when being upfront about what happened and why the story is false. Then move on. Avoid being defensive, but do not be secretive about it because secrecy will allow others to invent more stories about you to fill in the gaps.

4. Analyze the motive for spreading the rumor. Did you do something that could have been misinterpreted and can you change your behavior? Did the other person gain something by damaging your reputation? Make a plan to do something each day to reverse the impression have of you based on that malicious gossip.

5. If your actions have genuinely harmed another, make amends quickly and sincerely apologize..

6. Be conscientious about doing actively good deeds. Be consistent about it. Show others this is who you really are. Volunteer to genuinely help.

7. When you learn of somebody's bad reputation,

avoid adding to it. Do not spread that story.

8. Focus on accomplishing a goal. Then graciously share your victory with others so they can respect your achievement.

9. Evaluate your surroundings. Are you regularly associating with toxic people or situations? If you are, you may need to make a clean break and embrace a fresh environment.

Objective Achieved

Techniques for finding the truth despite being misled. Convince people of our true nature to overcome incorrect gossip.

Group Conversation

This is the proposed method for guiding a group in an open ended discussion of a topic. The same topic may explore different aspects with different audiences. Start with a question to get the group interacting. Make sure all parties can participate and vocalize their opinions about characters and situations. Remember to thank the group for their participation and opinions.

If a reputation of a company or country were damaged, what steps are needed to regain a good reputation?

After the host facilitates the following group

discussion questions (see below), the host may ask attendees to complete an optional homework assignment by the next meeting.

1. How would you graciously share and celebrate an accomplishment without bragging?

2. What would you do if you found out a lie was being spread about you?

3. Under what circumstances should you confront the person who is the source of the lies about you? How would you approach them? Why would you not approach them?

4. What activities that you undertake may make people assume you are one one way (good reputation) or another (bad reputation)?

5. Are you currently acting in a way that can be misinterpreted?

Assignments (Optional)

Document a person or group of people in history with a good reputation. List the actions they did which proves to you they earned their "good reputation"?

End of Conversation Station for this Book 1.

2 Book: AromaX 2030

Theme

Leadership.

Does leadership matter? In this story, there is a leadership change which has devastated the AromaX middle class, yet elevated the small upper class.

As a result of this sudden change, some citizens of AromaX are accepting and others are resisting.

Why might people in general resist leadership change?

In this book we are introduced to the corporate city of AromaX, where businesses used to profit off glamour, fashion, and fragrance.

This corporate city used to be ruled by the Mattick family, yet now, Otto Mattick is a lab assistant working under the authoritarian leadership of the aggressive and corrupt Twins.

In this story, the term **"Twins"** references a faceless power figure who replicated lies until lesser power figures copied that leader's brand or habits for the sole purpose of gaining power. Followers sacrificed their reputation, integrity, and boldly lied. The Twins encourage in-fighting for the leader's favor, back-stabbing, gas-lighting, and other destructive behaviors to obtain wealth and power at any cost. The theme "Leadership" asks us to evaluate the role of integrity and ethics in leadership roles. In what area of your life do you set an example or lead?

The backstory of Courtly City is that it used to be an American-style democracy, however a couple of belligerent or hostile people lied to convince a population to place them in charge.

Once the Twins obtained power over the people, they spread lies to retain that power, seize more land and wealth, and spread negative propaganda about the former leaders to prevent them from getting the people to restore the Mattick family to the throne. Instead of respecting agreements, the Twins used force to simply grab more land and power, yet they did not want the mundane task of establishing and enforcing laws and other mundane tasks to keep society functioning properly.

Courtly City was once a bankrupt town and auctioned off to the Courtly family. AromaX, on the other hand, had the Mattick leadership thrown out and disgraced unjustly.

If your land became bankrupt, would you trust a corporation to restore it? If your land had good leaders pushed out with lies, and the people were denied resources to make sure they never could rise up against those who stole power, what would you do? Would you remain or seek to leave? Why do you think refugees leave their homes? How would you lead to keep your citizens happy?

How has leadership impacted your life? Does the type of leadership of a country matter? Share examples with your group.

Chapters Referenced

Book 02 AromaX 2030

1 CHAPTER 04: (2030) AROMAX LAB: LINDEN & MATTICK ONE MONTH EARLIER-NO RESULTS 3

2 CHAPTER 05: (2030) AROMAX APARTMENT: OTTO MATTICK THAT EVENING SPEAKS WITH TOPLINER 26

3 CHAPTER 06: (2030) ISLAND LONGFELLOW: THE ISLAND RECRUITS STAND UP TO MEET LONGFELLOW 34

4 CHAPTER 07: (2030) COURTLY CITY: SARAH CONDO: SARAH AND GEORGIA HEAD TO TRAIN STATION TO GO OUT 65

Preparation for Group Structured Activities

Group leader will need: A virtual or physical place to write so audience can see the group notes. A way to interact with the audience. These activities can be assigned as homework or performed with an interactive group.

Structured Activity 1

Take one person aside from the group and provide feedback on a topic in a structured manner.

1. Tell that individual the topic of evaluation

2. Describe their specific actions or behavior you want to address.

3. State your objective observations on how that action, in your opinion, affected others.

4. Pause and ask that individual for their recollection of the events.

5. Provide easy-to-execute actions for how to modify the behavior (if their behavior had negative reactions) and how to amplify the behavior (if it had positive reactions).

6. Come to an agreement between the two of you regarding what steps will be taken by both of you moving forward. Explain the clear criteria which need to be achieved to get a small reward.

7. After both parties have achieved the agreed upon actions, there should be a reward issued for the accomplishment.

8. Make sure the reward given is equal to the task achieved. You do not want to give too large a reward. Also a reward can be genuinely praising that person in front of peers.

9. Make sure the reward is meaningful to the

person who is receiving it. That means that each person may need a different reward. A shy introvert will not like public praise. An extrovert may prefer public praise.

Structured Activity 2

10. List activities in your local community for which you can volunteer.

11. List others in your community you can encourage to join you in this volunteer activity.

12. What do you think you will need to do to be a good leader for those people?

13. If you learned of corruption (cheating) in your group, how would you address it to remove all motivation to cheat? What actions would you take to root out the cheating so it does not recur.

14. How does poor leadership promote harmful or ineffective results? What is the root cause and how do people react to poor leaders?

15. List examples of leadership where there was corruption and what you would do to eliminate that corruption so the group could be productive. List what the group could achieve with the corruption removed.

Objective Achieved

Understand the impact of effective leadership and how to treat those under your leadership.

Understand how poor or corrupt leadership has negative consequences.

Group Conversation

This is the proposed method for guiding a group in an open ended discussion of a topic. The same topic may explore different aspects with different audiences. Start with a question to get the group interacting. Make sure all parties can participate and vocalize their opinions about characters and situations. Remember to thank the group for their participation and opinions.

After the host facilitates the following group discussion questions (see below), the host may ask attendees to complete an optional homework assignment by the next meeting.

1. Every situation has good and bad people. How would you react if you were good, but you are forced to assume the identity of somebody who is bad?

2. What would you do if the only chance you had to escape from a bad situation required you to shed everything you knew, and to leave it behind?

3. Would you risk taking on a new identity of unknown origin?

4. Who in your life would realize you had been falsely accused and would come, therefore, to your aid?

5. What would you do if you were all alone and had to live with a bad reputation which was forced on you?

6. If you were a new leader, how would you convince the people to accept your leadership?

7. How would you instill confidence in your followers that you will consider their best interest in all your decisions?

8. How will you instill trust after they have had a bad leader?

9. If you lived through a difficult time, such as war, epidemic, pandemic, or economic depression, how would you encourage your neighbors to forge forward and create a better tomorrow?

Assignments (Optional)

1. Look up corrupt leaders in the news.

2. Document actions you could take to eliminate their corrupt influence.

3. Document the potential achievements of the people once that corruption was removed.

End of Conversation Station for this Book 2.

3 Book: Brio 2030

Theme

Destiny.

We rarely have control over our circumstances. We do have control over how we react to those circumstances.

How do you think the daily choices you make help create your future destiny?

In this book, we peek inside the culture of the underwater bubble city of Brio.

Is destiny comprised of the choices we make for ourselves?

Or is destiny the course we take, laid out for us by a wealthy powerful influence, which only allows us to take the path they want us to pursue?

Do others manipulate us to force us down that path, not giving us any choice?

Or have we shown we become overwhelmed with choice and are unable to make a wise decision for ourselves? Therefore, do we relinquish our power of choice to others?

Chapters Referenced

Book 03 Brio 2030

1 CHAPTER 08: (2030) COURTLY CITY: HOTEL: THE REAL OTTO MATTICK EXPLAINS TO TOPLINER- OFF TO THE TRAIN STATION 3

2 CHAPTER 09: (2030) COURTLY CITY: TRAIN STATION: GEORGIA & SARAH 20

3 CHAPTER 10: (2030) COURTLY CITY: ROAD: WATSON & TRES ON BUS OUT OF TOWN PLANNING FOR NEXT CON. BALLOON MONITORING. ZOR & LINDEN CALL WATSON UP TO CHECK ON OTTO MATTICK'S TRIAL 56

4 CHAPTER 11: (2030) BRIO: BJORN'S QUARTERS: BRIO & PAT SEEDS 80

5 CHAPTER 12: (2030) BRIO: GARDENS: BJORN & PAT SEEDS 90

6 CHAPTER 13: (2030) BRIO: GARDENS: BJORN LISTENS TO PAT SEED'S INSTRUCTIONS & THE LOCKED ROOM 103

Preparation for Group Structured Activities

Group leader will need: A virtual or physical place to write so audience can see the group notes. A way to interact with the audience. These activities can be assigned as homework or performed with an interactive group.

Structured Activity 1

Select five people in the news and describe what you believe they are destined to achieve or encounter. Support your hypothesis with factual events.

Did any of the people you selected contribute to a negative situation? Did they contribute to making a bad situation better? How?

Structured Activity 2

List why others may support or hinder what you believe to be your destiny.

List what you can do to encourage others to support you as you work toward your goal or destiny.

How do superficial elements influence how willing or unwilling people will be to support you?

Consider your general grooming, how you dress, the language you use when expressing yourself, etc.

Objective Achieved

Clarify what destiny is to you and how others perceive the term. Describe what you think you are destined to achieve and why.

Group Conversation

This is the proposed method for guiding a group in an open ended discussion of a topic. The same topic may explore different aspects with different audiences. Start with a question to get the group interacting. Make sure all parties can participate and vocalize their opinions about characters and situations. Remember to thank the group for their participation and opinions.

After the host facilitates the following group discussion questions (see below), the host may ask attendees to complete an optional homework assignment by the next meeting.

1. When did you first start thinking about your destiny or future?

2. How much do you think your natural talents contribute to your destiny vs. a skill you struggle to master?

3. Is your anticipated destiny formed by your choices or by the influence of those around you?

4. In your opinion, can destiny be changed or is it predetermined, therefore your actions cannot change it?

5. In Greek mythology three fates (**Moirai**-*Greek*/**Parcae**-*Roman*) assign destinies to mortals. In these fables, it is said their decisions were final and they were the authors of the Book of Fate. Which of these three fates do you resonate with the most and why?

a) **Clotho**: (the Spinner) She is spinning fate. She uses the thread of life and influences the present times.

b) **Lachesis**: (the Allotter) She is measuring the duration of a mortal's lifespan and influences future times. She is allotting blocks of time to humans to determine how long they will live on earth.

c) **Atropos**: (the Inflexible) She ends life abruptly. This fate has influenced the past.

According to Greek mythology, each fate is assigned the past (**Atropos**), the present (**Clotho**) or the future (**Lachesis**) of mortals on earth.

Assignments (Optional)

Interview five people and document their definition of "destiny" and what leads them to their definition.

Do you agree with the answers you collected? Why or why not?

End of Conversation Station for this Book 3.

4 Book: Courtroom 2031

Theme

Opportunity.

In this story, Bjorn's curiosity got him a new identity as well as blame for a crime he never committed.

Why?

The identity foisted upon Bjorn was associated with a man who may or may not have been framed for a crime...however Bjorn soon realized he himself was being framed for that crime.

Opportunity. Determination. Curiosity. Bjorn had all these traits. How did they help or hurt him?

What of Otto Mattick?

What opportunity do you see in your life? How will you know if you should take it or avoid it? What is the consequence of you selecting or avoiding this opportunity?

Chapters Referenced

Book 04
Courtroom
2031

1 CHAPTER 14: (2031) BRIO: COURTROOM: JURY & ZOR HEAR BJORN'S TESTIMONY 3

2 CHAPTER 15: (2031) BRIO: COURTROOM - ZOR EXPLAINS THE GAMES OF BRIO TO BJORN 13

3 CHAPTER 16: (2031) BRIO: COURTROOM: RECESS ENDS-TRIAL RESUMES 17

4 CHAPTER 17: (2031) BRIO: COURT: RESUMES 24

5 CHAPTER 18: (2030) BRIO: ESCAPE POD: PAT AND BJORN TRY TO ESCAPE FROM BRIO 46

Preparation for Group Structured Activities

Group leader will need: A virtual or physical place to write so audience can see the group notes. A way to interact with the audience. These activities can be assigned as homework or performed with an interactive group.

Structured Activity 1

Opportunity. Determination. Curiosity. Blame.

Identify how these words relate to each other. Does

one cause another or are they sequentially ordered?

Write one sentence per word which is a personal action statement you can take in your own life.

Structured Activity 2

Write regarding how you would explain to another person how to identify and respond to an opportunity?

Can you create an "opportunity"? If yes, how?

Can you glean anything good out of a "bad opportunity"? How would you do that?

Objective Achieved

Defining, responding to and handling consequences of an opportunity we may encounter.

Group Conversation

This is the proposed method for guiding a group in an open ended discussion of a topic. The same topic may explore different aspects with different audiences. Start with a question to get the group interacting. Make sure all parties can participate and vocalize their opinions about characters and situations. Remember to thank the group for their participation and opinions.

After the host facilitates the following group discussion questions (see below), the host may ask attendees to complete an optional homework assignment by the next meeting.

1. How would you react to being blamed for something you had nothing to do with?

2. Once a reputation is damaged, what can you do to get your good name back?

3. How would you assist a friend who was accused of a bad thing?

4. What would you do to investigate the facts and aid in restoring the reputation?

5. Why do you think "your good name" or reputation is valuable?

6. Why is slander and liable considered bad things?

Assignments (Optional)
Document one famous quote per word. :
1. *Opportunity.*
2. *Determination.*
3. *Curiosity.*
4. *Blame.*

End of Conversation Station for this Book 4

5 Book: Chaos 2030 to 2031

Theme

Chaos.

Who gains power in a chaotic environment? Is it the aggressive bold vocal person who claims they are the only solution and can resolve the problems causing chaos? Does chaos exist because the masses are complacently allowing a corrupt leader to "get away with it"?

Is it our obligation to speak up and step up to set events back on track?

The word "chaos" has been in use since the 1300's to mean a gaping empty void of immeasurable space. This could mean any situation where one does not see a solution.

Some people do gain status, power, and even wealth by taking advantage of a chaotic situation. Sometimes it is easier to tear down than to build something up.

Evaluate why AromaX recruits wanted to train and join Longfellow and Warren in distant lands? What hope do they provide?

Do you know of somebody who spread gossip

which was not fact-checked, meaning they are spreading lies about something?

If there is a negative chaotic event in the real world, how do you research what actions caused this event? Who profits from things being chaotic in that situation? How can the chaos be removed and normal structure restored? Who has the power to do that? What can you do?

Chapters Referenced

Book 05 Chaos 2030-2031	1 CHAPTER 19: (2030) ISLAND: LONGFELLOW TESTS THE COMM RANGE WITH DOGS AND WARREN PULLS HIM OUT OF A HOLE 3
	2 CHAPTER 20: (2031) ISLAND: LONGFELLOW'S FOREST RUN FOR MEN- CUFFLINKS & BOWTIES & BURST TECH 20
	3 CHAPTER 21: (2031) BRIO: POD: BJORN IN THE POD SWIMS WITH FISHES 26
	4 CHAPTER 22: (2030) COURTLY CITY: SARAH CONDO: CHASE THE CHICKEN WITH GEORGIA 46
	5 CHAPTER 23: (2031) COURTLY CITY: HIGH SCHOOL: SARAH ON AN AFTER CLASS DATE 58

Preparation for Group Structured Activities

Group leader will need: A virtual or physical place to write so audience can see the group notes. A way to interact with the audience. These activities can be assigned as homework or performed with an interactive group.

Structured Activity 1

Is the news today filled with chaos?

Identify two elements of chaos in a specific news stories.

Structured Activity 2

How would you define a "whistle-blower"?

How does the whistle-blower contribute to resolving chaos?

Objective Achieved

Defining *behaviors which contribute* to confusing chaos.

Defining *actions which can resolve* a chaotic situation.

Group Conversation

This is the proposed method for guiding a group in an open ended discussion of a topic. The same topic may explore different aspects with different audiences. Start with a question to get the group interacting.

Make sure all parties can participate and vocalize their opinions about characters and situations. Remember to thank the group for their participation and opinions.

After the host facilitates the following group discussion questions (see below), the host may ask attendees to complete an optional homework assignment by the next meeting.

1. What should be done to remove the elements of chaos from a situation?

2. How would one handle those who seem to stir up chaotic events?

3. How should one interact with people who enjoy drama and enjoy causing roller-coaster events around them?

4. Have you ever encountered a person who relishes the power of generating havoc?

5. How would you explain to somebody that true power is clearing up confusion, not causing it?

6. How does one provide succinct clarity in a foggy confusing environment?

7. How do we forge a forward moving path so all people can succeed in a win-win collaborative situation?

8. Describe "zero sum" situations where only one party can win and for them to win, another party must lose?

9. How might your actions and responses possibly contributing to a chaotic environment?

10. Do you take the time to research a story to determine if it is true and based on fact before sharing it with others so you build a reputation for being truthful?

11. Do you investigate the root cause of why a situation is the way it is?

12. Can you identify any persons or organizations that would benefit from a public chaotic event? Think of epidemics, pandemics, natural disasters, economic downturns or depressions. How do you separate those organizations that can help during these difficult times from those who gouge and profit from these situations? Would you change anything? Why or why not?

Assignments (Optional)

Find news stories and build a strategy which answers these question:

1. Define the goal. What did that party, group, corporation, or army gain by taking over another group?

2. What is needed to take advantage of that situation and seize control against the will of the group.

3. Now that the group, which seized power during a time of chaos, is in control, what skills are needed to govern and maintain the infrastructure so the people are willing and happy to remain and cooperate with the new leadership?

4. Compare the characteristics.

a) List characteristics needed to seize control

b) List characteristics needed to govern cooperatively with the people

c) How are these different?

d) Can the same group execute both activities? why or why not?

End of Conversation Station for this Book 5.

6 Book: Dolphin Express 2031

Theme

Pride.

"Pride comes before a fall" is a theme from Proverbs 16:18 in the Bible.

In this book, we see how pride, hubris and charging forth led to destruction, or "a fall".

Bjorn felt guilty that his actions caused so much harm.

Do you think Bjorn caused Brio to fall, or do you think Bjorn was just in the wrong place at the wrong time? Was it only a matter of time before Brio collapsed and Bjorn, in fact, is blameless?

Would you experience "survivor's guilt" if you were in Bjorn's situation?

Survivors guilt is defined as the feeling a survivor battles when they realize they have survived a devastating situation while others did not. Perhaps, the survivor believes, they did not do enough to save the others, who were more worthy and should have survived.

Chapters Referenced

Book 06 Dolphin Express 2031

1 CHAPTER 24: (2031) COURTLY CITY: FANCY RESTARUANT: SARAH AND MARK DATE 4

2 CHAPTER 25: (2031) COURTLY CITY: HIGH SCHOOL BREAK ROOM & CAFÉ: SARAH AND THE WILBUR DATE 28

3CHAPTER 26: (2031) COURTLY CITY: LIBRARY: SARAH INTRODUCES GEORGIA TO LIBRARY AND MRS. LIBRIS AND WATSON 52

4 CHAPTER 27: (2031) ISLAND: SHORE: BJORN ON LAND 65

5 CHAPTER 28: (2031) ISLAND: SHORE: BJORN WAKES UP AFTER ISLAND NAP & GETS SLOBBERED 75

6 CHAPTER 29: (2031) ISLAND: VILLAGE: LONGFELLOW APOLOGIZES TO THE LOCAL VILLAGE MAN 87

Preparation for Group Structured Activities

Group leader will need: A virtual or physical place to write so audience can see the group notes. A way to interact with the audience. These activities can be assigned as homework or performed with an interactive group.

Structured Activity 1

List modern situations where a person may suffer from survivor's guilt.

List ways to help somebody suffering from survivor's guilt.

Structured Activity 2

Write the difference between having pride in your work to do your very best and having arrogant pride which leads to boasting, bragging, exulting in your own accomplishments and flattering oneself with a swagger while demeaning the achievement of others.

Pride in my work	Arrogant boasting

Objective Achieved

Recognizing the behavior of those who inappropriately esteem themselves.

How to support somebody with survivor's guilt.

Group Conversation

This is the proposed method for guiding a group in an open ended discussion of a topic. Start with a question to get the group interacting. Make sure all parties can participate and vocalize their opinions about characters and situations. Remember to thank the group for their participation and opinions.

After the host facilitates the following group discussion questions (see below), the host may ask attendees to complete an optional homework assignment by the next meeting.

1. Do you ever wonder why you were given a chance when perhaps somebody you believe is more worthy than you was not? How do you handle that?

2. How do you balance needing to take care and pride in your work to develop quality output compared to being too prideful?

3. Would blind pride prevent you from seeing "red flags" or warnings that you might be hurting another party with your ambition?

4. How would you justify harming an innocent person as a "cost of doing business" so you meet your goal at any cost?

5. How would you handle situations if innocents inadvertently were harmed and you had not intended this?

6. What would you do - if anything- to make restitution to the injured parties?

Assignments (Optional)

Interview a person with these scenarios and document their responses.

1. Present a scenarios where the interviewee is attaining a goal where the only way to get that goal would harm innocents. Would they choose, or refuse, to harm others?

2. Present a scenario where the goal is attained by deceit. If the deception is discovered, the interviewee would lose their goal. Which would they choose? Risk losing the goal and admitting to the deception or doing what they can to keep the secret from being revealed?

3. Present a scenario where the interviewee has the attained the goal by chance or accident. They are praised for the grand achievement which would normally come from hard work and dedication. Would the person accept the praise or would they admit that it was obtained by chance and the reward may rightfully belong to somebody else?

End of Conversation Station for this Book 6.

7 Book: Rough-N-Ready 2031

Theme

Goals.

How do you meet a goal you cannot see?

How do you form goals? How do you plan to reach goals?

If the goal seems too overwhelming, are we able to break it down into such tiny steps that we can do something each day to reach that goal?

How do you reach a goal which is not based on objective skill?

Chapters Referenced

Book 07 Rough-N-Ready 2031	1 CHAPTER 30: (2031) ISLAND: HEADQUARTERS: LONGFELLOW PONDERS THE CONTENTS OF HIS BOX 3
	2 CHAPTER 31: (2031) ISLAND: SHORE: BJORN AND THE DOGGIE 21
	3 CHAPTER 32: (2031) ISLAND: SHORE: BJORN MEETS HIS FURRY FRIENDS AGAIN 24
	4 CHAPTER 33: (2031) ISLAND: HEADQUARTERS: BJORN WAKES UP IN A HOUSE 28

5 CHAPTER 34: (2031) ISLAND: HEADQUARTERS: LONGFELLOW TRIES TO GET BJORN TO LEAVE 39

6 CHAPTER 35: (2032) ROUGH-N-READY: THEATER: OTTO MATTICK –ROUGH-N-READY AND SLASH/ PERCY SNATCHER 45

7 CHAPTER 36: (2031) AROMAX: LAB: LOU POLE LINDEN CAN MAKE A MAGSOL 54

Preparation for Group Structured Activities

Group leader will need: A virtual or physical place to write so audience can see the group notes. A way to interact with the audience. These activities can be assigned as homework or performed with an interactive group.

Structured Activity 1

1. Describe a goal you wish to accomplish within 12 months.

2. List the people you need to help you achieve that goal

3. List the financial resources and other supplies needed to meet your goal

4. List what you will have to achieve in 6 months to be on track to attaining the goal in 12 months.

5. List what you will have to achieve in 3 months to be on track to attaining the milestone at 6 months.

6. List what you will have to achieve by the end of your first month to be on track to meet the milestone at 3 months.

7. List what you need to accomplish by the end of your first week.

8. List the minimal action you will need to do every day to meet your end of week milestone.

Structured Activity 2

9. Design a visual to check off your monthly milestones as they are achieved.

Example:

1	2	3	4	5	6	7	8	9	10	11	12
✓											

Objective Achieved

Defining a goal and clarifying the steps needed to achieve that goal.

Group Conversation

This is the proposed method for guiding a group in an open ended discussion of a topic. The same topic may explore different aspects with different audiences. Start with a question to get the group interacting. Make sure all parties can participate and vocalize their opinions about characters and situations. Remember to thank the group for their participation and opinions.

After the host facilitates the following group discussion questions (see below), the host may ask attendees to complete an optional homework assignment by the next meeting.

Sarah, in this story dated two men, only to find both of them lacking in qualities which would encourage her to spend time with them again.

1. If you are trying to forge a relationship and cannot control the circumstances, nor the inventory of options, what would you do?

2. Would you compromise your values? Would you re-evaluate your values to see if you are being too exclusionary?

3. Would you stay the course and try to do something which would welcome more options for you to evaluate?

4. Would you not think about it and simply go with whoever shows you attention even if you did not value the character of that person?

Assignments (Optional)

Name a person or group which have achieved a goal you admire?

How can you use this individual or group achievements as an inspirational role model to help you achieve your goals?

⭐⭐ �឴✺✵ ⭐⭐

End of Conversation Station for this Book 7.

8 Book: Lab 2031 to 2032

Theme

Innovation.

Nothing can be developed in a corrupt environment. To create and inspire, you must be in a place where you can take chances, fail, try again, and refine with the support of a trustworthy network, environment, or team.

If there is corruption in the mix, the person below the corrupt individual will model their behavior for those who rank below them. If corruption is at the highest levels, it will trickle down and be difficult to remove.

The word *innovacion* came into use around the mid 1400s. It meant restoration and renewal. Around the 1540s, the concept of innovation has meant discovery.

"Innovation" essentially means the development of a new and unique change resulting from experiments to establish a new useful element.

In this story, Dr. Lou Pole Linden wants to create, yet he is threatened by the intellect and creativity of Otto Mattick, who used to be part of the ruling family. Jealousy and a lust for ambitious power has motivated

Dr. Linden to belittle Otto Mattick so that he is forced to be in a place which is clearly beneath the doctor. Instead of collaborating and partnering with each other, Dr. Linden's emotions are willing to obscure one of his most valuable assets because there is a chance that Otto Mattick is better than Linden and this infuriates Linden.

Linden is willing to spite and hurt his own future to ensure Otto Mattick never gets recognition even if it is objectively deserved.

For Linden, this is a price he is willing to pay, a risk he is willing to take, to preserve his own ego and obtain his goal by compromising an objectively ethical code.

By contrast, Sarah Paradise has demonstrated selfless resourcefulness by improvising with the limited tools she has available blended with her creative wits to fix problems of others. For example, Sarah ponders a strawberry gardening problem shared by a fellow instructor, Mr. Element. Sarah is intent on finding a solution.

Her mindset is to see how she can help others as her compassion is honed from her personal experiences of being denied certain things capriciously.

In the series EDGES, Sarah was punished by the Administrators for bringing her class on an authorized field trip to Library. She was removed from her elementary-grade level classroom and immediately transferred to teach at a high school without any preparation. Her credits were severely reduced and she had to give up her Comm, or communication device. Sarah's "crime" was that the field trip to Library, although approved by parents and Administrators, was now being capriciously considered a violation with consequences.

Sarah surmised it must have been because the information contained in the paper books contradicted the digital information put forth recently by the Administrators in an attempt to rewrite history.

She always tries to empathize with the motives of another person. Sarah does have boundaries established by her code of ethics. She recognizes when her character does not align with the ethics of another. She knows when she must part ways and sever relationships.

Until cutting ties, Sarah is always willing to give a second chance. Even-though, Georgia Peach is opposite to Sarah Paradise's more subdued nature, Sarah sees some good in Georgia and is always hoping for the best.

Chapters Referenced

Book 08 The Lab 2031-2032

1 CHAPTER 37: (2031) AROMAX: LAB: LOU POLE LINDEN SELECTS A CRATE, OPENS IT, MAKES A LIST 4

2 CHAPTER 38: (2031) AROMAX: LAB: LOU POLE LINDEN EXPLAINS TO THE HOMELESS TEST SUBJECTS 8

3 CHAPTER 39: (2031) AROMAX: LAB: LOU POLE LINDEN BEGINS THE MOLD FOR THE FIRST OF THREE EXOSKELETONS 14

4 CHAPTER 40: (2031) AROMAX: LAB: LOU POLE LINDEN SCOLDS HIS CHILDISH GUESTS 17

5 CHAPTER 41: (2031) AROMAX: LAB: LOU POLE LINDEN PROPOSES THE NANONEVEL 21

6 CHAPTER 42: (2030) AROMAX: LAB: LOU POLE--LINDEN NANO NEVEL IS COOKING 35

7 CHAPTER 43: (2032) COURTLY CITY: HIGH SCHOOL: SARAH LISTENS TO VIRGINIA HAMM LESSON PLANS & PROMOTES TAKING SIDE JOBS 44

8 CHAPTER 44: (2032) COURTLY CITY: HIGH SCHOOL: GEORGIA INFORMS SARAH, MR. ELEMENT'S STRAWBERRIES & PARTY: 62

Preparation for Group Structured Activities

Group leader will need: A virtual or physical place to write so audience can see the group notes. Also required is a way to interact with the audience. These activities can be assigned as homework or performed with an interactive group.

Structured Activity 1

- Corruption
- Innovation
- Code of ethics

1. List two ways that corruption stops innovation.

2. List two ethical codes of conduct which supports innovation.

3. List actions you can personally take to support the ethics which support innovation.

4. List actions you can personally take to stop corruption.

Structured Activity 2

Provide examples of bad outcomes resulting from corrupted activities being accepted as valid:

    a) Corrupt scientific experiments

    b) Corrupt elections

    c) Corrupt corporate management

    d) Corrupt government policies such as bribery, kleptocracy, and antitrust schemes.

    e) Contraband smuggling by local, state, and federal prison officials in exchange for bribe payments.

Objective Achieved

Students understand how to identify corruption and how to take actions to support ethical innovation instead.

Group Conversation

This is the proposed method for guiding a group in an open ended discussion of a topic. The same topic may explore different aspects with different audiences. Start with a question to get the group interacting. Make sure all parties can participate and vocalize their opinions about characters and situations. Remember to thank the group for their participation and opinions.

After the host facilitates the following group discussion questions (see below), the host may ask attendees to complete an optional homework assignment by the next meeting.

1. What is an acceptable price of innovative?

2. Is it acceptable to compromise your ethical values?

3. Is it acceptable to try and grab unearned credit?

4. What characteristics in another person will tell you when to cut ties with that person because of their corrupt behavior?

5. How much will we risk to obtain our envisioned goal?

Assignments (Optional)

Write a paragraph stating what kind of risk you will personally take to obtain an ethical and honorable goal.

Describe at least one behavior you may encounter which will be corrupt enough for you to abandon your goal so that you may retain your integrity.

In your opinion, how does ethics support innovation and how does corruption hurt or hinder innovation?

End of Conversation Station for this Book 8.

9 Book: Strawberry EarthShake 2032-2033

Theme

Ingenuity.

Being resourceful means to take your existing resource (or ordinary object) and making it work for a valuable purpose for which it may not have originally been designed.

To be considered ingenious, one must have capability, brilliance, the ability to see an object and evaluate many other uses for it.

The ingenious person should posses creative intelligence, gumption, discernment, and dedication to resolving the problem.

In this story, we see Dr. Lou Pole Linden interact with the Test Subjects which were inside the box which arrived at the AromaX lab in 2031.

The manner in which the Test Subjects arrived demonstrates the low value Linden places on them. He needs them, but views them as disposable.

He is demonstrating that he is willing to cross the lines of ethical conduct to exploit Test Subjects for his NanoNevel experiment. He views himself as ingenious, but he is also willing to violate moral and ethical conduct to achieve his goals.

Chapters Referenced

Book 9 Strawberry EarthShake 2032- 2033

1 CHAPTER 45: (2032) COURTLY CITY: HIGH SCHOOL: SCHOOL PRACTICE PARTY, TRIP TO THE DRUNKEN STRAWBERRIES 3

2 CHAPTER 46: (2032) COURTLY CITY: HIGH SCHOOL: MR. ELEMENT IS SURPRISED AT THE STRAWBERRY PATCH & EARTHSHAKE 29

3 CHAPTER 47: (2033) ISLAND: VILLAGE: FEVER AMONG RECRUITS. LONGFELLOW LESSON 41

4 CHAPTER 48: (2033) ISLAND: HEADQUARTERS: LONGFELLOW ASKS ABOUT THE TREES 67

5 CHAPTER 49: (2033) ROUGH-N-READY: THEATER: STAGE:OTTO MATTICK AND TOPLINER SHOW   72

Preparation for Group Structured Activities

Group leader will need: A virtual or physical place to write so audience can see the group notes. A way to interact with the audience. These activities can be assigned as homework or performed with an interactive group.

Structured Activity 1

Write down one ordinary household object. List how many different ways you can use it productively besides it's intended use.

Compare your list with others in your group and discuss the results.

Structured Activity 2

Are you aware of how your actions impact others around you, or are you oblivious to hurting others in your pursuit of your "ingenious goal"?

Write three ways an inventor may hurt others in the pursuit of completing an invention.

Write at least one way you, as that inventor, could still achieve your goal without hurting others. How might that change your outcome?

Is it in the inventor's control to conduct experiments without hurting others? Why or why not?

Objective Achieved

Be aware that the actions an inventor takes to pursue a goal may affect others.

Group Conversation

This is the proposed method for guiding a group in an open ended discussion of a topic. The same topic may explore different aspects with different audiences. Start with a question to get the group interacting. Make sure all parties can participate and vocalize their opinions about characters and situations. Remember to thank the group for their participation and opinions.

After the host facilitates the following group discussion questions (see below), the host may ask attendees to complete an optional homework assignment by the next meeting.

1. Describe how ingenuity and innovation and invention are different?

2. Can you view yourself as "ingenious" or is that a title bestowed upon you by others, and why?

3. How would you practice honing the skill of using objects around you as tools?

4. How is parkour different from gymnastics? Describe how one uses objects in the outside world, and one uses a gym. What is the best way to learn and practice parkour?

5. Can you list the downside of being ingenious?

6. Describe how you might take ordinary objects and repurpose them to solve a specific problem?

7. Will others appreciate your efforts, or will they resent your talent if you are successful in developing a

creative way to solve a problem? Why?

8. Is it worthwhile to imagine how to use an object for something other than its intended purpose? Why?

9. How many different ways can a paperclip be used? Do not say to clip pieces of paper together. Think of ingenious ways a paperclip can be used as a tool.

10. Can you take your current skills and think about a different area of life in which such abilities would be valuable, or even applicable?

Assignments (Optional)

Select one group question (from previous page) or use the example below. Write a paragraph answering that question.

For example: If a person were trained in the military to do one specific task, how would that skill transfer to the civilian world? Write about the talents which are needed to execute a military skill well, and think about how those talents could be reapplied. Do not think of the skill itself, rather think about what is needed to be good at that skill.

For example, if a person in the military is an expert sharp shooter, they need good eyesight. What civilian occupations also need good eyesight?

End of Conversation Station for this Book 9

10 Book: Narci 2033

Theme

Narcissism.

In this book, the term "Narci" is defined as a slang term for a person who may be so enamoured with their own importance that they assume the world around them has been created to serve them.

It refers to a person who feels entitled to manipulate and even hurt those around them because those other people are disposable and can always be replaced.

The person enveloped in narcissistic tendencies are so self-assured that they may not realize the harm they do and the one-way loyalty they demand.

They will be oblivious to problems around them, which prevents them from solving those problems early while small issues can still be managed. This means they are usually surrounded by "cliff-hangers" and drama.

They struggle with what is real versus their own created reality, where they are the most important.

They, however, view themselves are being the only solution to any problem, and therefore they must be worshiped at all costs. The slang term "Narci" has then been reduced to "RC", simply because saying the letters sounds like the word "Narci" in English.

Narcissism was first used around 1905 in Germany. The word was *Narzissismus..* Some may have abbreviated the term to be *"Narzi"*. It was a word created by a German psychiatrist Paul Näcke (1851-1913), around the year 1899. He wrote his observations in 1898 when commenting on a work by Havelock Ellis. The topic was about the Greek mythological character *Narkissos..*(Ovid, "Metamorphoses," iii.370)

This fable was about a handsome young man who became entranced and fell in love with his own reflection in the placid still waters.

A nymph named Echo loved him, yet he did not return Echo's affections and instead longed to see his own reflection and was willing to sacrifice relationships with others, included a devoted Echo.

As a result of his self-admiration he was turned into a flower called a narcissus.

The figure of "Narcissus" appeared in literature again in 1767. Samuel Taylor Coleridge, a poet and leader of the British Romantic movement born in 1772, used the word in a letter from 1822, where he wrote: *"Of course, I am glad to be able to correct my fears as far as public Balls, Concerts, and Time-murder in Narcissism."* In this sense, he uses the word "Narcissism" to mean "excessive love or admiration of oneself."

Chapters Referenced

Book 10 Narci 2033

1 CHAPTER 50: (2033) COURTLY CITY: LIBRARY: SARAH AT LIBRARY LOOKING FOR SUMMER JOB & EARTHSHAKE AFTERMATH 3

2 CHAPTER 51: (2033) COURTLY CITY: LIBRARY: SARAH TELLS MRS. LIBRIS SHE IS ON WAITLIST FOR COURTLY JOB 14

3 CHAPTER 52: (2033) ISLAND: HEADQUARTERS: LOCATION ON HIB. BJORN LEARNS LISTENING NARCI BEFORE MISSION TALK DURING MORNING EXERCISE 17

4 CHAPTER 53: (2033) COURTLY CITY: HIGH SCHOOL: GEORGIA SLIPS OUT OF MISS VIRGINIA HAMM'S SCHOOL OFFICE 57

5 CHAPTER 54: (2033) COURTLY CITY: HIGH SCHOOL: SARAH GET'S BLAMED BY MISS HAMM FOR GEORGIA'S SNOOPING 62

6 CHAPTER 55: (2033) COURTLY CITY: SARAH CONDO: SARAH CONFRONTS GEORGIA ABOUT GETTING FRAMED 72

Preparation for Group Structured Activities

Group leader will need: A virtual or physical place to write so audience can see the group notes. A way to interact with the audience. These activities can be assigned as homework or performed with an interactive group.

Structured Activity 1

Write one paragraph about a situation you have encountered with a narcissistic personality and how you handled it.

If you have not encountered a narcissist, then list the characteristics of the "Narci" or "RC" described in the book, and how you would handle a person like that.

Structured Activity 2

Think of one public figure. Check off how many narcissistic characteristics they evidence from the list below. (Note this is not a scientifically derived list.)

1. ☐ - The person becomes very angry when their honor has been offended, in their opinion. They may even be offended if accuses of being a narcissist.

2. ☐ - They blame others for doing something wrong, be it real or imagined, trying to make the other person feel shame so no blame will fall on them. They can present themselves as both victim and bully.

3. ☐ - They do not appear to care about how another person feels. They do not empathize. They find it exhausting and annoying to be required to feign caring about another person.

4. ☐ - They boast of their skills and never admit

deficiencies.

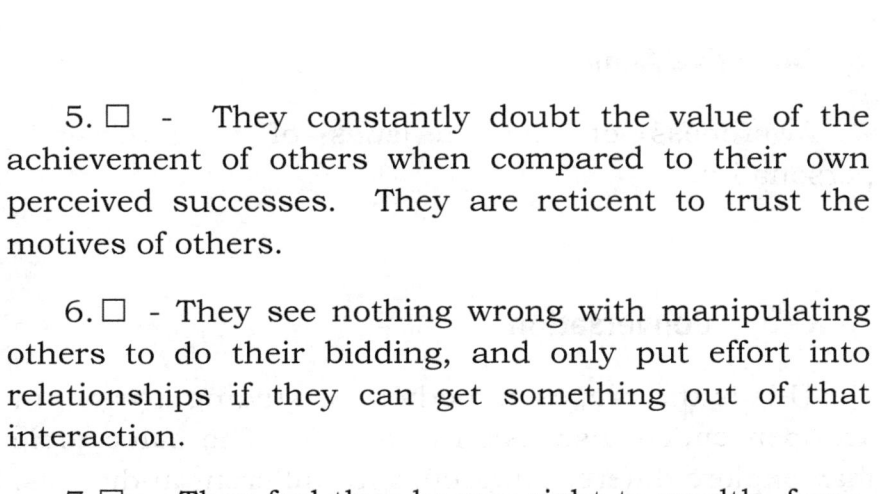

5. □ - They constantly doubt the value of the achievement of others when compared to their own perceived successes. They are reticent to trust the motives of others.

6. □ - They see nothing wrong with manipulating others to do their bidding, and only put effort into relationships if they can get something out of that interaction.

7. □ - They feel they have a right to wealth, fame, recognition, admiration, acclaim or success even if they have not put forth effort. If they do obtain a goal and it hurts somebody along the way, they view it "as a necessary cost of doing business." They, therefore, feel they should not be held accountable for their harmful actions. They may mock and belittle others.

8. □ - They crave praise and admiration. They enjoy bragging about their "accomplishments" and enjoy showcasing their expertise.

9. □ - The narcissist rarely reciprocates favors unless that favor will manipulate the other person to get the narcissist what they want.

10. □ - They enjoy taking attention-grabbing risks without heeding consequences.

Objective Achieved

Awareness of characteristics of a narcissistic personality.

Group Conversation

This is the proposed method for guiding a group in an open ended discussion of a topic. The same topic may explore different aspects with different audiences. Start with a question to get the group interacting. Make sure all parties can participate and vocalize their opinions about characters and situations. Remember to thank the group for their participation and opinions.

After the host facilitates the following group discussion questions (see below), the host may ask attendees to complete an optional homework assignment by the next meeting.

1. How should you behave if you encounter a narcissistic personality?

2. How do you tell if person is a narcissist?

3. What characters in the book express narcissistic personality traits?

4. Do you think a narcissistic personality would ever get depressed? Why?

Assignments (Optional)

Create a list of characteristics which are narcissistic.

Create a list of warning signs to know if somebody is expressing narcissistic tendencies.

Write a paragraph about how can you handle these personality types if you encounter them in a business setting, in a personal setting, in your home-life?

If you have any narcissistic characteristics yourself, what actions will you take to change or why will you not change?

End of Conversation Station for this Book 10.

11 Book: Lock 2033 to 2034

Theme

Impostor Syndrome vs. creating a new identity.

A person may need to "reinvent" themselves in order to distance their future from a tainted past. They may need a fresh start with a fresh occupation in a fresh environment.

This need to create a new identity is different from wrestling with the "Impostor syndrome", where the person feels like a guilty survivor who should not have survived.

In this case, when creating a new identity, the person focuses on nothing but survival. They realize they cannot live as their old selves and must experience a new self.

"Impostor syndrome" may also be experienced if a person achieves something, yet does not quite believe it was they who deserved the rewards for that achievement.

In these cases, one must evaluate when that person must come to terms and say "Yes. I did do this on my own merit. I should behave as if I have achieved it and stop downplaying the importance of the achievement." At times one must say "This is what I do and I do it well."

Chapters Referenced

Book 11 The Lock 2033-2034

1 CHAPTER 56: (2033) ROUGH-N-READY: THEATER: APARTMENT: OTTO MATTICK LECTURES TOPLINER ON RIGHT AND WRONG 3

2 CHAPTER 57: (2034) ROUGH-N-READY: THEATER: DRESSING ROOM: OTTO MATTICK TRIES TO CONVINCE THEATER MANAGER TO LET THEM TAKE THEIR ACT ON TOUR. OTTO TELLS TOPLINER TO STAY PUT. 13

3 CHAPTER 58: (2034) ROUGH-N-READY: THEATER: STAGE: TOPLINER SHARES HIS INFORMATION 17

4 CHAPTER 59: (2034) ROUGH-N-READY: THEATER: STAGE: OTTO MATTICK COVERS FOR TOPLINER AND MANAGER GIVES WARNING 26

5 CHAPTER 60: (2034) ISLAND: HEADQUARTERS: LONGFELLOW GIVES BJORN A NEW ID AND SHOWS TALLMAN'S BOX TO CONVINCE BJORN TO JOIN WARREN PIECE ON MISSION 33

6 CHAPTER 61: (2033) COURTLY CITY: LIBRARY: MRS. LIBRIS SHARES HER PHILIPPIANS BOOK WITH SARAH. MAN BURSTS INTO LIBRARY & INTRODUCES HIMSELF & OFFERS SUMMER JOB. 52

Preparation for Group Structured Activities

Group leader will need: A virtual or physical place to write so audience can see the group notes. A way to interact with the audience. These activities can be assigned as homework or performed with an interactive group.

Structured Activity 1

Write the difference between confidence and arrogance.

Write the advantages and disadvantages of displaying characteristics of confidence versus arrogance if you are a certain age, or sex, or from a certain social class.

Do you think the attitudes of the general public, assuming these differences are based on age, sex and social class, should or could change?

Structured Activity 2

List reasons why people need to create a new identity.

List reasons why people may experience the "Impostor syndrome" even if they have genuinely achieved something of worth. What would you do to help them recognize their valid achievement?

List how you personally would take action to totally change the view others have about you.

Objective Achieved

Recognize traits of "Impostor Syndrome" in another person and how to help them acknowledge their genuine achievement.

Group Conversation

This is the proposed method for guiding a group in an open ended discussion of a topic. The same topic may explore different aspects with different audiences. Start with a question to get the group interacting. Make sure all parties can participate and vocalize their opinions about characters and situations. Remember to thank the group for their participation and opinions.

After the host facilitates the following group discussion questions (see below), the host may ask attendees to complete an optional homework assignment by the next meeting.

1. Share a time when you or somebody you knew experienced "Impostor Syndrome"?

2. How did you recognize "Impostor Syndrome?"

3. How would you help somebody overcome "Impostor Syndrome"?

4. What is the difference between arrogance and conceit, versus recognizing that you have the skills to achieve a valid goal with confidence?

5. How would you structure a process to announce an award-winning achievement in a way which is fair to all participants in the contest without diluting the "first prize win"?

6. How would an arrogant narcissistic person respond to being accused of narcissism ?

7. List reasons why a person may need to create a new identity?

8. How would a person change the undesirable impression others have about them?

Assignments (Optional)

Write a paragraph about a society which dismisses the genuine achievement of a social demographic. What is that society missing out on by not acknowledging that demographic's achievement? What could you do to help genuine achievements be recognized?

✫✫   ✲⚝✲   ✫✫

End of Conversation Station for this Book 11.

12 Book: Village 2033 to 2034

Theme

Home.

Home is usually defined as a fixed residence, where you can safely keep your personal belongings. It was used in Hamlet by Shakespeare around the 1550s.

The slang term, "Make yourself at home", meaning to make yourself comfortable in a place where you do not live was used around 1892. In the 1510's, "home" was used as a term to mean being "at ease".

In 1841, the horse racing term "home stretch" was first used.

In 1856 the term "home base" was used in baseball.

In 1867, the term "home plate" was also used in baseball.

In 1869, the term "home team" in sports was used.

In 1907, the term "nothing to write home about", was meant to describe an unremarkable ordinary thing.

In 1914, a song popularized the phrase, "keep the home fires burning". This means "wait for me".

In 1955, the term "home field advantage" was used in sporting events.

Chapters Referenced

Book 12 The Village 2033-2034

1 CHAPTER 62: (2033) AROMAX: OUTSKIRTS SHELTER: FEMALE1 & MALE1 JOIN THE AROMAX CAMP—ELDER JAMES ANNOUNCES PLANS TO BUILD A VILLAGE 5

2 CHAPTER 63: (2034) COURTLY CITY: BARN: SARAH'S JOB AT THE OVERFLOW BARN STABLES FIRST DAY 14

3 CHAPTER 64: (2033) AROMAX: OUTSKIRTS SHELTER: AROMAX FEMALE1 & MALE1 SP GUARD GENE VOLUNTEERS DURING FINAL CONSTRUCTION OF HOMELESS VILLAGE 31

4 CHAPTER 65: (2034) COURTLY CITY: BARN: SARAH AT THE HORSE AUCTION- HERE IS GEORGIA PEACH DURING FINAL DAYS OF OVERFLOW BARN SUMMER JOB 43

5 CHAPTER 66: (2034) NUREMBERG : WARREN & BJORN ARRIVE IN GERMANY- NUREMBERG WINTER & MUSIC BOX 59

6 CHAPTER 67: (2034) COURTLY CITY: SARAH'S CONDO: SARAH & GEORGIA COOK AT SARAH'S PLACE. SARAH CONFRONTS GEORGIA AS TO WHY SHE TOOK THE WATSON JOB, BEEN AVOIDING SARAH, AND NOW SUDDENLY WANTS TO BE FRIENDS 74

Preparation for Group Structured Activities

Group leader will need: A virtual or physical place to write so audience can see the group notes. A way to interact with the audience. These activities can be assigned as homework or performed with an interactive group.

Structured Activity 1

List the different types of "homes" where people live in your country.

Which one do you live in and which do you prefer to live in?

Structured Activity 2

List what you can do to make somebody feel comfortable and welcomed in your home.

How would you welcome somebody who was forced out of their home against their will and is looking for a new place to establish roots.

Objective Achieved

Understand that the term "home" has nuanced meaning for different demographics.

Group Conversation

This is the proposed method for guiding a group in an open ended discussion of a topic. The same topic may explore different aspects with different audiences. Start with a question to get the group interacting. Make sure all parties can participate and vocalize their opinions about characters and situations. Remember to thank the group for their participation and opinions.

After the host facilitates the following group discussion questions (see below), the host may ask attendees to complete an optional homework assignment by the next meeting.

1. Define what makes "home" for you.

2. Why do you feel comfortable in a place?

3. Do you view "home" as a happy place or a place you want to avoid going back to? Why?

4. What is the difference between "home", and a place where all your belongings are stored?

5. What is the one thing which may remind you of a cozy comforting place when you are away in a new place? For example, is there an aroma, sound, or object which remind you of when you were little?

6. Do you ever feel displaced as if you did not belong somewhere? Why did you feel that way?

Assignments (Optional)

List elements which make you feel comfortable and remind you of a happy time in your life.

List elements which made you feel as if you did not belong.

Compare those lists. Write what actions can you take to reduce the experiences of "not belonging" and increase the reminders of a happy time in your life?

End of Conversation Station for this Book 12.

13 Book: Cologne 2034

Theme

Legacy.

What will be the legacy we leave behind that others will remember?

Is the goal for others to remember us or is it for others to remember the thing which improved their lives because of our actions?

Some may be so focused on survival: where to sleep, live, and what to eat. These survival necessities prevent focusing on leaving a legacy.

What can we achieve today? Is it OK if we achieve nothing other than survival?

Can we learn from the good or bad legacy others have left us?

Chapters Referenced

Book 13
Cologne
2034

1 CHAPTER 68: (2034) COURTLY CITY: OPEN AIR MARKET: SARAH BUYS A SCREEN AND OSI. GEORGIA EXPLAINS 5

2 CHAPTER 69: (2034) COLOGNE: WARREN & BJORN ARRIVE IN GERMANY-COLOGNE CITY 20

3 CHAPTER 70: (2034) COLOGNE: IN GERMANY WARREN PIECE SENDS BJORN TO VIENNA, AUSTRIA TO LEARN TO DANCE FOR THE MISSION. BJORN REJECTS THE NARCI'S ADVANCES 36

4 CHAPTER 71: (2034) COURTLY CITY: LIBRARY: SARAH AND MRS.   LIBRIS-SCREEN IN HAND 51

5 CHAPTER 72: (2034) VIENNA: TRAIN & STUDIO: BJORN ARRIVES IN VIENNA, AUSTRIA- MEETS DAN SER 59

6 CHAPTER 73: (2034) VIENNA: STUDIO: BJORN: FIRST DANCE LESSONS WITH DAN SER 70

7 CHAPTER 74: (2034) AROMAX: GUARD GENE RETURNS TO HOMELESS VILLAGE & THE PROMISE 84

Preparation for Group Structured Activities

Group leader will need: A virtual or physical place to write so audience can see the group notes. A way to interact with the audience. These activities can be assigned as homework or performed with an interactive group.

Structured Activity 1

List something you would like to create, which would still be around 100 years from today.

Structured Activity 2

How can you help somebody else create something which will benefit people in the future?

What skills are you able to contribute today and what skills do you hope to learn to help achieve this "legacy"?

Objective Achieved

Understand small actions today can have a lasting "legacy" years from now.

Group Conversation

This is the proposed method for guiding a group in an open ended discussion of a topic. The same topic may explore different aspects with different audiences. Start with a question to get the group interacting. Make sure all parties can participate and vocalize their opinions about characters and situations. Remember to thank the group for their participation and opinions.

After the host facilitates the following group discussion questions (see below), the host may ask attendees to complete an optional homework assignment by the next meeting.

Gone Book 26 Conversation Station- Book 14

1. Do you want to be remembered for something good or something bad?

2. Do you want to create or build something, or take down a bad thing? What is that thing?

3. If you had all the resources to help you with your goal, what is the one thing you want to change in your immediate geography this week?

4. If you know what needs to be changed in your area, do you think you can write a plan regarding how to change that thing and then present that plan to somebody in charge to help them get started on executing that plan?

5. This chapter was about Cologne. Describe your favorite scent.

6. What components do you think are needed to create a fragrance?

Assignments (Optional)

Select your favorite fragrance and identify the components of that fragrance. What are the key ingredients which appeal to you?

Write one sentence describing the legacy you may want to leave for future generations.

End of Conversation Station for this Book 13.

14 Book: Dress for the Ball 2034

Theme

Anticipation.

Yearning for a desire, a wish to come true can distract us from our responsibilities. Yes, we need a goal, but if that consumes us and we become lustfully addicted to that goal, perhaps it is no longer a goal, but an obsession.

What is the reason we get excited about obtaining something? Is the act of getting that magical thing satisfying? Why or why not?

In this story, Georgia wants Sarah to accompany her to a party. Why do you think Georgia wants to attend this function and why does she want Sarah Paradise to join her?

Is Georgia's enthusiasm contagious?

When you get enthusiastic about an upcoming event, how do others react to your enthusiasm?

Chapters Referenced

Book 14 Dress for the Ball 2034

1 CHAPTER 75: (2034) AROMAX: LAB:LOU POLE LINDEN GETS A VISIT FROM SOLDIER POLICE– MALE2 DOESN'T KNOW IF HE'S A GONNER 4

2 CHAPTER 76: (2034) AROMAX: OUTSKIRTS SHELTER: MALE2 ARRIVES AT HOMELESS VILLAGE CAMP 21

3 CHAPTER 77: (2034) COURTLY CITY: SP STATION: GUARD GENE LOSES LOU POLE LINDEN & HIS CHANCE OF PROMOTION TO DETECTIVE 27

4 CHAPTER 78: (2034) COURTLY CITY: SP STATION: SAMMY MEETS GENE 36

5 CHAPTER 79: (2034) COURTLY CITY: HIGH SCHOOL: BREAKROOM: GEORIGA AND SARAH AT SCHOOL 39

6 CHAPTER 80: (2034) COURTLY CITY: GEORGIA'S PLACE: SARAH BORROWS GEORGIA'S DRESS 44

7 CHAPTER 81: (2030) VIENNA: STUDIO: BJORN PERFECTS DANCING ALONG WITH DAN SER. BJORN GETS A PACKAGE. WARREN PIECE WILL SOON ARRIVE. 51

8 Chapter 82 (2034) VIENNA: STUDIO: BJORN DEMONSTRATES; WARREN PIECE ARRIVES TO SEE DAN SER & HOLE IN THE BARRIER 54

9 Chapter 83 (2034) VIENNA: STUDIO: BJORN & WARREN GET A MESSAGE FROM LONGFELLOW BEFORE THEY HEAD TO THE VIENNA STATE OPERA BALL 64

10 Chapter 84: (2034) WATSON MOUNTAIN MANSION: SARAH & GEORGIA AT THE SNOWY ECHO PARTY CHECK THEIR COATS. 70

Preparation for Group Structured Activities

Group leader will need: A virtual or physical place to write so audience can see the group notes. A way to interact with the audience. These activities can be assigned as homework or performed with an interactive group.

Structured Activity 1

Identify and describe local fashions which would be appropriate for a "dance" or "formal outing". Describe how you feel getting dressed up for a special occasion.

Structured Activity 2

List the traits somebody may express if they are excited or have anticipation about an upcoming event.

What is the reason, in your opinion, this person may be filled with yearning and anticipation.

Describe the difference, in your opinion, between anticipation and obsession.

Objective Achieved

Identify what characters do to prepare for an important event.

Group Conversation

This is the proposed method for guiding a group in an open ended discussion of a topic. The same topic may explore different aspects with different audiences. Start with a question to get the group interacting. Make sure all parties can participate and vocalize their opinions about characters and situations. Remember to thank the group for their participation and opinions.

After the host facilitates the following group discussion questions (see below), the host may ask attendees to complete an optional homework assignment by the next meeting.

1. How do we stir desire in others? How can our enthusiasm be contagious so others also get excited?

2. How is creating desire in others different from marketing or propaganda?

3. Each of the characters in the story has an important event. Not all events require dressing formally. How do we know the event is important to each of these characters?

    a) Sarah and Georgia attend a ball

    b) Guard Gene makes an arrest of Lou Pole Linden

    c) Sammy Scribe introduces himself to Guard Gene.

    d) Male2 survives an experiment and find a home.

    e) Bjorn and Dan prepare for an event.

4. If there is a function and somebody is not invited, how would you react to that person?

5. How would you provide encouragement for

somebody to be their best?

6. How do we make our presence welcomed so others look forward to seeing us again?

7. How do our actions make another person happy or smile?

8. How do we avoid making people tired of us?

9. Why do some people cling to mementos of others to remember them in their absence? Photos, symbols?

Assignments (Optional)

List ways one can create a yearning for our return?

List ways you can show somebody you want to see them again.

End of Conversation Station for this Book 14.

15 Book: Mountain Mansion 2034

Theme

Fate.

A fatalistic person believes that what will be will happen regardless of any actions they take. A term used since the late 14th century, *"fate"* means "one's lot or destiny; predetermined course of life."

Those who believe they are the masters of their own lives believe that their future is fully determined only by their actions and they do not blame circumstances for their situation.

Most people are in between.

Most people believe they cannot control some circumstances, but realize their actions do contribute to the outcome of some others.

For example, if you never study for a test, chances are you will not pass the test.

So a fatalistic person will not see the point to studying because regardless of what they do, they believe they will still either pass or fail the test based on their destiny.

By contrast, the opposite pragmatic path will state they will dedicate effort to study. If they did their best and they still fail, they may think they did not study hard enough. The outcome is tied to their actions and personal effort expended.

The middle-ground is somebody who studies, yet if they fail, they understand some things are outside of their control.

Both the pragmatic personality and the middle-ground personality will put effort into studying for the next test to increase their chances of success.

The fatalistic person, by contrast, may not study because they leave the test results to fate.

The back of book 15 reveals the bark of a tree, yet there appears to be a face. The artist explained that the face symbolizes a happy element within us all, which comes out in our work. What we produce contains traces of our personality. This means if we focus on having an attitude of integrity and ethics, and wish to generate a smile in those who use the our creations, then that spirit will be apparent in our final product.

Bottom line is, do you believe that what you do matters and has an impact?

Chapters Referenced

Book 15 Mountain Mansion 2034

1 CHAPTER 85: (2034) WATSON MOUNTAIN MANSION: ECHO INTIATES & SARAH FINDS GEORGIA & SEES BJORN GET PULLED OFF DANCE FLOOR. GEORGIA TAKES SARAH OFF THE FLOOR. 5

2 CHAPTER 86: (2034) VIENNA: AUSTRIA OPERA HOUSE: AFTER WARREN PIECE PULLED BJORN OFF THE DANCE FLOOR 12

3 CHAPTER 87: (2034)WATSON MOUNTAIN MANSION: CONTROL ROOM: SARAH GETS ACCUSED OF BEING GEORGIA & WATSON GOES MISSING 17

4 CHAPTER 88: (2034) WATSON MOUNTAIN MANSION: CONTROL ROOM: WHY ARE THOSE SCREENS BLANK? 27

5 CHAPTER 89: (2034) VIENNA: FLYING MACHINE: BJORN AND WARREN PIECE GET TO ROUGH-N-READY 31

6 CHAPTER 90: (2034) WATSON MOUNTAIN MANSION: CONTROL ROOM: SARAH & GEORGIA LEAVE CONTROL ROOM & SARAH GETS ACCOSTED 35

7 CHAPTER 91: (2034) ROUGH-N-READY: FLYING MACHINE LANDS: BJORN AND WARREN PIECE GET TO ROUGH-N-READY 41

8 CHAPTER 92: (2034) WATSON MOUNTAIN MANSION: PSL SHACK: SARAH GETS MISTAKEN FOR GEORGIA 45

9 CHAPTER 93: (2034) ROUGH-N-READY: STREETS: BJORN AND WARREN GET TO ROUGH-N-READY THEATER & MEET STREET PREACHER 51

Preparation for Group Structured Activities

Group leader will need: A virtual or physical place to write so audience can see the group notes. A way to interact with the audience. These activities can be assigned as homework or performed with an interactive group.

Structured Activity 1

Write how a fatalistic mind-set impacts cheating versus studying.

Structured Activity 2

Write a paragraph which describes how you, in the role of a coach to a team sport, must coach a team where half the players are fatalistic and half are pragmatic.

How would you coach each group to prepare or win the upcoming game?

Objective Achieved

You will be able to explain the motives behind decisions different people make (pragmatic vs. fatalistic).

Group Conversation

This is the proposed method for guiding a group in an open ended discussion of a topic. The same topic may explore different aspects with different audiences. Start with a question to get the group interacting. Make sure all parties can participate and vocalize their opinions about characters and situations. Remember to thank the group for their participation and opinions.

After the host facilitates the following group discussion questions (see below), the host may ask attendees to complete an optional homework assignment by the next meeting.

1. Do we have the ability to focus on making the right choices despite overwhelming odds? Should we try and alter our own destiny?

2. How much of our actions are determined by fate and the circumstances we cannot control?

3. Can we impact the destiny of others?

4. Describe how both a fatalistic person and a pragmatic person will prepare for a sports game?

Assignments (Optional)

Write one paragraph on "destiny". What circumstances outside of your control impact one's destiny.

Write a description about what motives a fatalistic person versus a pragmatic person. Will the fatalistic person feel as if they make an impact on anything? Will the pragmatic person feel they must always be in control of the outcome?

What factors inside your control impact destiny.

What do you believe is your personal destiny?

End of Conversation Station for this Book 15.

16 Book: Investigate 2034

Theme

Investigate.

Why should you exercise the skill of "critical thinking" and investigate hypothesis to prove whether or not they are factual and true? Some may call this the "scientific method".

Both the questioning of your hypothesis, and investigating with applying the scientific method, are ways of logically collecting and organizing evidence so that you can make careful observations and informed decisions.

You can create an assumption, or hypothesis, and then test it to see if it is true or false. Then you can take that process and apply it to future similar situations to estimate the outcome.

In this story, Sarah Paradise is compelled to investigate something. What do you think motivates her to discover the truth?

Chapters Referenced

Book 16
Investigate
2034

1 CHAPTER 94: (2034) WATSON MOUNTAIN MANSION: PSL SHACK: SARAH FINDS OF WHAT SHE IS ACCUSED 4

2 CHAPTER 95: (2034) ROUGH-N-READY: BJORN & WARREN LEAVE THE PREACHER AND HEAD INTO THE THEATER 14

3 CHAPTER 96: (2034) WATSON MOUNTAIN MANSION: PSL SHACK: SARAH STILL IN WATSON'S GUARD SHACK 22

4 CHAPTER 97: (2034) ROUGH-N-READY: THEATER: DINING ROOM: BJORN & WARREN HEAR BJORN'S NAME CALLED FROM ON STAGE 31

5 CHAPTER 98: (2034) WATSON MOUNTAIN MANSION: PSL SHACK: SARAH IS HELD IN WATSON'S PSL GUARD SHACK. 35

6 CHAPTER 99: (2034) ROUGH-N-READY: THEATER: DINING ROOM: BJORN & WARREN ...HEAR SOMETHING 43

7 CHAPTER 100: (2034) WATSON MOUNTAIN MANSION: GROUNDS: SARAH INVESTIGATES WATSON'S STUDY 49

8 CHAPTER 101: (2034) ROUGH-N-READY: STREETS: BJORN & WARREN FOLLOW ZOR 59

9 CHAPTER 102: (2034) WATSON MOUNTAIN MANSION: INSIDE HOUSE: SARAH & PSL 69

10 CHAPTER 103: (2034) ROUGH-N-READY: STREETS: TOPLINER & OTTO MATTICK FOLLOW BJORN ESTERDAY & WARREN PIECE 77

Preparation for Group Structured Activities

Group leader will need: A virtual or physical place to write so audience can see the group notes. A way to interact with the audience. These activities can be assigned as homework or performed with an interactive group.

Structured Activity 1

Write a hypothesis you wish to investigate.

Hypothesis:_____

    1. What caused this?

    2. What is connected to this?

    3. What effect does this have on something else?

Objective Facts:

    1. Fact: _____

    2. Fact: _____

    3. Fact: _____

Question:

    1. What parameters (or boundaries) are needed to make the hypothesis true?

_____

_____

_____

2. For how many iterations must I ask this question before I get enough answers which are consistently aligned with the truth?

_____

Conclusion:

Based on the results of my experiment, the hypothesis under investigation appears to predicts that in the future: _____

Structured Activity 2

Who else in your group investigated the same hypothesis and came up with the same conclusion?

Who came up with a different conclusion? Do they have evidence to support their conclusion? Are your two different conclusions complimentary or contradictory?

Which conclusion is objectively factual by supporting repeatable evidence?

Note 1: "repeatable evidence" means you can replicate all the steps to come out with the same conclusion.

Note 2: "supporting evidence" means there are facts which are objective and support the ultimate conclusion. This gives your experimental results credibility.

Objective Achieved

Identify unproven hypothetical assumptions vs. proven hypothesis with repeatable evidence supporting a conclusion.

Group Conversation

This is the proposed method for guiding a group in an open ended discussion of a topic. The same topic may explore different aspects with different audiences. Start with a question to get the group interacting. Make sure all parties can participate and vocalize their opinions about characters and situations. Remember to thank the group for their participation and opinions.

After the host facilitates the following group discussion questions (see below), the host may ask attendees to complete an optional homework assignment by the next meeting.

1. Why does Sarah Paradise feel compelled to find the real culprit?

2. If you learn of gossip, are are told something, how do you know if it is factual or false?

3. List types of topics for which you can use the Scientific Method of investigation.

4. Why not just accept things as they are presented to you, and don't try to "find the truth"?

5. Do you think Sarah Paradise used the "scientific method" to come to a factual conclusion?

6. Are you curious?

7. Do you need to know the reason why an action transpired? Do you require supporting evidence?

8. Do you echo and repeat what others may have told you without verifying evidence to support their information?

Assignments (Optional)

Find a news story and investigate if it is true. Use the Scientific Method and cite sources.

You may use information available to you at your local library, in an encyclopedia, or other resources at your disposal.

End of Conversation Station for this Book 16.

17 Book: Stasis 2034

Theme

Stasis.

Waiting. Do you feel trapped as if in suspended animation? Is there a time when you feel as if you are in a "holding pattern" or that you must "stay the course"?

Sometimes a period of inactivity is called "rest". It allows us to revive and refresh ourselves. At other times, however, some may assume we are being "lazy".

Stasis actually means "standing still". In this story, what stands still?

Around 1745 the term "stasis" meant a "stoppage of circulation". It has also been used to describe a political stand-still. Some used it to indicate the condition of anything which is motionless. Others used the term to reference a party, or a sect, with seditious goals. "Sedition" was a concept from the 15th century which meant "tending to incite treason."

Chapters Referenced

Book 17 Stasis 2034

1 CHAPTER 104: (MARCH 2030) ROUGH-N-READY: BJORN & WARREN DISCOVER ZOR'S PLACE 4

2 CHAPTER 105: (2034) ROUGH-N-READY: TOPLINER & OTTO MAKE IT BACK ON STAGE 7

3 CHAPTER 106: (2034) WATSON MOUNTAIN MANSION: STUDY: SARAH GETS A SNOWY TOUR, THEN DEDUCTIVE REASONING ABOUT THE UNKNOWN VISITOR WHO WAS IN WATSON'S STUDY 10

4 CHAPTER 107: (2034) ROUGH-N-READY: THEATER: APARTMENT: TOPLINER AND OTTO AFTER THE SHOW 26

5 CHAPTER 108: (2034) AROMAX: OUTSKIRT SHELTER: LOGO IN TOWN 32

6 CHAPTER 109: (2034) WATSON MOUNTAIN MANSION: STUDY: SARAH EXPLAINS the BED SHEETS 38

7 CHAPTER 110: (2034) ISLAND: HEADQUARTERS: DAN SER WARNS LONGFELLOW 43

8 CHAPTER 111 (2034): WATSON MOUNTAIN MANSION: BEDROOM: SARAH & PSL VISIT THE TWIN BEDS 52

9 CHAPTER 112: (2034) ROUGH-N-READY: ZOR'S PLACE: INSIDE ZOR'S BUILDING: MAP MATCHES. TRAIN ARRIVES 56

10 CHAPTER 113 : (2034): WATSON MOUNTAIN MANSION: STUDY: SARAH BACK AT THE WATSON STUDY:- DOES SHE FIGURE IT OUT? 62

11 CHAPTER 114 : (2034): ROUGH-N-READY: ZOR'S PLACE: BJORN AND WARREN EXPLORE THE STASIS PODS 72

Preparation for Group Structured Activities

Group leader will need: A virtual or physical place to write so audience can see the group notes. A way to interact with the audience. These activities can be assigned as homework, or performed with an interactive group.

Structured Activity 1

1. Describe: a **semantic memory**, which is the memory of general knowledge or fact. For example, describe what a book looks like.

2. Describe: an **episodic memory** where you recall an episode in your life, such as a time when you slipped and fell. You remember where you were, who was there, and what happened to cause the fall.

3. Describe: an **emotional memory** where you felt something, such as distress. This memory can trigger anxiety if you were to see something which reminds you of the time (or episode) in which you fell. Others around you may not understand why you suddenly feel distressed because they do not recognize the trigger.

4. Describe: **"muscle memory"** (procedural memory) or something you can do automatically because you have physically done it repeatedly, (such as breathing).

Structured Activity 2

Now, in the event of a trauma or an upsetting experience, how will each of these memories be impacted?

1. Describe how facts gathered during semantic memory can be scattered and thereby preventing the brain from forming a full picture?

2. Describe how one or two episodes might be recalled in fragments and out of order?

3. Describe how emotional traumatic memories could be triggered unexpectedly?

4. Describe how routine actions (procedures) get interrupted because you unconsciously recall an event which leads to an experience of pain.

5. Do you think that a person who does not understand why they are experiencing these responses may turn to some form of stasis to seek relief?

6. Would a person who experienced a trauma be a good witness to testify about that traumatic event in court?

7. What is the best way to interact with somebody who has experienced trauma?

Objective Achieved

Awareness regarding how to treat people who have experienced trauma and why they may turn to "standing still", or stasis, to cope.

Group Conversation

This is the proposed method for guiding a group in an open ended discussion of a topic. The same topic may explore different aspects of that topic with different audiences. Start with a question to get the group interacting. Make sure all parties can participate and vocalize their opinions about characters and situations. Remember to thank the group for their participation and opinions.

After the host facilitates the following group discussion questions (see below), the host may ask attendees to complete an optional homework assignment by the next meeting.

1. What might cause us to become inactive for a period of time?

2. What might trigger us to "lay low" or "catch our balance" if something happened which unsettled us?

3. In this story, what do the characters discover is being held "in stasis"?

4. Ask yourself, how does the term "stasis" apply to your own life?

5. Under what circumstances might stasis be a good thing, or a bad thing?

Assignments (Optional)

Document the best way to recognize somebody who has experienced trauma. List the best ways to respond to them and encourage their healing.

End of Conversation Station for this Book 17.

18 Book: Realize 2034

Theme

Realize.

Realization can be defined as the act of being aware that a condition is coming into genuine existence, or is being manifested.

An example would be if a person had an idea to start a project and then got all the people and resources needed to execute that project. That project is becoming a reality, and is, in fact, being realized.

Realization can also apply to yourself. How would you behave if you were in a situation for which you felt unsuited? On the other hand, how would you react if you realized you did have all the skills or resources needed to handle this situation, after all?

In this story, Sarah realizes there is more to her teaching co-worker, Georgia, than she originally had assumed.

In addition, in this story, Sarah realizes the PSL's true motives for consulting her.

Also, Female1 realizes she is more than her circumstances of being homeless. She used to be an employed accountant and she reminds herself that she is, in fact, a trained, skilled, professional with talents which could help alleviate the dismal situation she and her companions faced. Female1 may, in fact, have all the skills she needs to protect herself and her impacted community.

Sammy Scribe and Guard Gene realize there is more going on than they had originally thought. They realize they need to collaborate to get to the truth.

Topliner Mattick and Otto Mattick also realize what Zor has really been up to, and how many others were harmed in the process of Zor and Watson's lust for profits.

This story is about each character's realization of their "aha moments" when they discover the pieces of a puzzle have now come together.

Chapters Referenced

Book 18 Realize 2034

1 CHAPTER 115: (2034) WATSON MOUNTAIN MANSION: STUDY: SARAH SEES PSL'S TRUE MOTIVES 4

2 CHAPTER 116: (2034) COURTLY CITY: SP STATION: SP PARKING LOT IN COURTLY CITY 8

3 CHAPTER 117: (2034) WATSON MOUNTAIN MANSION: GROUNDS: GEORGIA & SARAH ESCAPE 11

4 CHAPTER 118: (2034) AROMAX: OUTSKIRTS HOMELESS SHELTER. PLAN TO DRAIN ACCOUNTS 22

5 CHAPTER 119: (2034) WATSON MOUNTAIN MANSION: FLYING MACHINE: SARAH GETS ANSWERS 28

6 CHAPTER 120: (2034) AROMAX: BUS STOP: FEMALE1 RECALLS HER ACCOUNTING PAST AT THE BANK 34

7 CHAPTER 121: (2034) AIR: WATSON MOUNTAIN MANSION: FLYING MACHINE: GEORGIA AND SARAH TALK IN THE AIR 39

8 CHAPTER 122: (2034) ROAD TO WATSON MOUNTAIN MANSION: MOUNTAIN ROAD: DO SAMMY AND GUARD GENE GET TO THE ESTATE? 55

9 CHAPTER 123: (2034) AIR: LEAVING WATSON MOUNTAIN MANSION: FLYING MACHINE: GEORGIA REVEALS HER REAL REASON FOR GETTING CLOSE TO WATSON 60

10 CHAPTER 124: (2034) ROUGH-N-READY: TOPLINER & OTTO ENTERING ZOR'S BUILDING 68

11 CHAPTER 125: (2034) ROUGH-N-READY: ZOR'S PLACE: BJORN AND WARREN HIDE BEHIND A COFFIN TO AVOID THE MATTICKS 71

Preparation for Group Structured Activities

Group leader will need: A virtual or physical place to write so audience can see the group notes. It is also a way to interact with the audience. These activities can be assigned as homework, or performed with an interactive group.

Structured Activity 1

Read the questions below.

Select one character from the book.

Then, with that character in mind, write how that character responds for each question.

I have chosen to respond for character:_____

1. Why did it take your character this long to become aware and realize what is really going on?

2. Was your character blind to warning signs?

    a) If you believe the answer is "Yes, my character ignored warnings", then document those warning signs which were missed by your character.

    b) If you believe the answer is "No. My character paid attention to warnings", list the warning signs your character noticed. Describe if you think your character reacted wisely or not.

3. Was the truth concealed from your character?

a) If you believe the answer is "Yes. The truth was hidden from my selected character", then document what the character could have done to recognize the truth sooner. Who concealed the truth from your character and what was their motive?

b) If you believe the answer is "No. The truth was very clear all along and not concealed from my selected character", then what explains the character's action or inaction?

4. Did your selected character realize the truth in this book or in an earlier book? Describe the events or situation which revealed the truth to your character?

5. Do you identify with your character? What traits do you admire in your selected character? What traits do you dislike in your selected character?

6. Should your character actively try to control and change circumstances, or should your character passively accept what is happening around them without resistance? How might the choice impact their future?

7. Describe what motivates your character. Describe the way your character tends to communicate. For example, consider these personality traits: shy, passive, logically analytical, emotionally intuitive, practical, frivolous, friendly and personable, honest, manipulative, aggressive, or assertive, etc.

Structured Activity 2

Complete this chart. Use it later for your own reference.

	Question	Your Response
1	State a goal. Describe actions you can take to achieve that goal.	
2	Describe the actions you can take to change an uncertain future into a certainty.	
3	List how you can deal with an existing issue in your life today. How will you get the help you may need to cope with that issue?	
4	Write a statement which expresses appreciation for the positive things in your life. How will you use this statement as a reminder of the good in your life when you are feeling low?	

	Question	Your Response
5	Select one of these negative emotions that you experienced in the last week: impulsive, fearful, quick tempered, hateful, guilty, frustrated, anxious, or being unsure of your own capabilities. List a possible root cause for this negative feeling.	
6	How might you control or "let go" of your negative feelings? What should you do regarding the person, people or circumstances which hurt you or contributed to your negative feeling?	
7	How might you demonstrate happiness? Do you indulge in feeling silly, playful, or cheerful? What is your attitude toward wholesome fun?	

	Question	Your Response
8	Which form of exercise do you enjoy? How frequently do you participate in your favorite exercise? Can you commit to more frequent exercise? (Example: walking, dancing, swimming, running, weight lifting, gardening, etc.)	
9	List healthy foods you enjoy eating. How will you ensure you are only eating when you feel happy and hungry? Can you commit to avoid eating if you are upset, bored or not hungry?	
10	List the elements in your life you are powerless to influence. Describe how you can ask God (as you understand a Higher Power) for the insight, wisdom, and will to handle those events which are outside of your control.	

	Question	Your Response
	How might you release your anxieties so you may reach your full potential?	
11	If you were given one year from today onward of free choice and unlimited funds, what activities would you want to do in that time? What percentage of that time would you spend relaxing?	
12	What did you realize about yourself after you completed answering the previous eleven (11) questions?	

Objective Achieved

Recognize the impact of each person's decisions and the consequences of those choices on yourself and others.

Group Conversation

This is one proposed method for guiding a group through an open-ended discussion of a topic. The same topic may explore different aspects of that topic with different audiences. Start with a question to get the group interacting. Make sure all parties can participate and vocalize their opinions about characters and situations. Remember to thank the group for their participation and opinions.

After the host facilitates the following group discussion questions (see below), the host may next ask attendees to complete an optional homework assignment by the next meeting.

1. How would you react if you finally got the answer to a question which could not be answered previously? If relieved, why?

2. Describe situations where uncovering the truth is a good thing?

3. Describe situations where uncovering the truth is a bad thing?

4. How should a person react if they discovered they were betrayed by somebody they had trusted?

5. If somebody establishes a pattern of untrustworthy behavior, should you assume you are immune from their deceptions, or should you assume it will simply be a matter of time before you yourself are stung by their antics? Can you trust that person? Why or why not?

6. If you decide to forgive, then under what circumstances do you continue the relationship, or when do you determine to abandon the relationship?

7. What are the boundaries of forgiveness, and

when do you choose to never forgive?

8. In the "Did You Know" section, various types of governments were defined. Which one do you think would be the most successful and why? Which one do you live in today? If you were to lead a country, which form of government would you set up and why?

9. This book has an extra "Did You Also Know" section. This referenced elements which would build trust and tear it down. What tips could you take and apply to your personal life? Do you agree or disagree with these observations? If you followed these tips would your personal relationships improve?

Assignments (Optional)

Write a letter to somebody who has offended you, and therefore you have decided never to speak to them, again.

If you have offended somebody, write a letter of apology to them.

If you believe you have not offended another nor has anybody offended you, write a letter describing actions you will take to make the world better for somebody else.

End of Conversation Station for this Book 18.

19 Book: Impact 2034

Theme

Impact.

Which of your own decisions could make an impact on others?

The concept of an impact was used around the 1500s to mean pressing closely to something. The concept of striking forcefully was first recorded in 1916. The figurative image of having a forceful effect on something else was used around 1935.

What does the concept of "impact" mean to you? Is it negative, positive or a neutral term, in your opinion?

In this story, Georgia Peach and Sarah Paradise make a literal impact. This impact was not something Sarah had planned on.

Have you ever been surprised by events which have swept you in a direction you had not intended? Were you called upon to draw on talents and skills you thought you may not have needed?

Chapters Referenced

Book 19 Impact 2034

1 CHAPTER 126: (2034) AIR: FLYING MACHINE: GEORGIA CONFESSES SHE UNLOCKED IT 5

2 CHAPTER 127: (2034) YEAR 2034: ROUGH-N-READY: ZOR'S PLACE: BJORN MEETS OTTO- PODS UNLOCK 29

3 CHAPTER 128: (2034) AIR: SARAH & GEORGIA'S ROUGH DESCENT 35

4 CHAPTER 129: (203x) AIR: SARAH & GEORGIA & THE LANDING 39

5 CHAPTER 130: (2034) ROUGH-N-READY: ZOR'S PLACE: DOGS BARK OUTSIDE ROUGH-N-READY WAREHOUSE 43

6 CHAPTER 131: (2034) COURTLY CITY SPS NOTICE FLYING CRAFT & EXPLODE IT 52

7 CHAPTER 132: (2034) ANCOR ROAD: THE ANCORS GET THE SIGNAL 58

8 CHAPTER 133: (2034) HUB TRAIN STATION MILES AWAY FROM COURTLY CITY: SARAH AND GEORGIA IN THE HUB STATION SEE THE HORIZON BURST INTO FLAMES 63

Preparation for Group Structured Activities

Group leader will need: A virtual or physical place to write so audience can see the group notes. A way to interact with the audience. These following activities can be assigned as homework or performed with an interactive group.

Structured Activity 1

1. Document the safety steps you need to follow to keep your body safe from a sudden impact.

2. Document the psychological techniques you use to keep your mind and heart safe from harmful emotional impact.

3. Explain how healing occurs for you.

Structured Activity 2

1. Document a few examples about how PTSD, Shell Shock, and/or traumatic impact were handled throughout history?

2. Compare how some societies viewed a person who had experienced trauma in the past compared to the way that person would be viewed by that society today?

3. Share your opinion regarding the best way to help somebody (real or fictional) who has experienced trauma.

4. Describe with whom you want to share a vision of inspiration.

5. Describe how you will achieve a result by improving relationships and processes, without micromanaging. How will you discern you have appropriately involved your opinions in the improvement process?

a) **FULL RESPONSIBILITY** - Will you consult with your conscience and then will you announce orders to others, delegate and then leave the results to others?

b) **INDIVIDUAL OPINION**- Will you seek input from other individuals and consider all points of view and then announce your own decision?

c) **GROUP CONSENSUS**- Will you seek opinions from groups of people and collectively vote or come to some understanding as a group?

d) **FULL DELEGATION**- Will you delegate to other people the task of investigating facts, seeking opinions, and then making a decision trusting another person to act on your behalf?

6. Describe how you will facilitate agreement between two parties.

7. Describe how you will encourage others to be their best and celebrate their accomplishments.

Objective Achieved

Understand the relationship of the term "impact" to explain the interdependence of people upon each other.

Group Conversation

This is the proposed method for guiding a group in an open ended discussion of a topic. The same topic may explore different aspects of the topic with different audiences. Start with a question to get the group interacting. Make sure all parties can openly participate and vocalize their opinions about characters and situations. Remember to thank the group for their participation and opinions.

After the host facilitates the following group discussion questions (see below), the host may ask attendees to complete an optional homework assignment by the next meeting.

1. Do you get impatient if something does not happen quickly enough? How do you express or contain that impatience?

2. Do you feel as if your small decisions will never amount to any significant change? Describe an action which may result in a big change.

   a) For example, Smelling smoke, then calling the fire department and saving a building full of people.

3. Give an example in which a small action produced a positive impact or consequence.

4. What is one great way to make a positive or productive impact on another person's life? Why?

Assignments (Optional)

Read John Donne's 1624 Meditation 17 from *Devotions upon Emergent Occasions.*

Describe how the concept one person able to impact a group of people translates into how your actions can impact the lives of others. What do these words mean to you? Do they may you feel more or less important?

No man is an island,
Entire of itself,
Every man is a piece of the continent,
A part of the main.
If a clod be washed away by the sea,
Europe is the less.
As well as if a promontory were.
As well as if a manor of thy friend's
Or of thine own were:
Any man's death diminishes me...

End of Conversation Station for this Book 19.

20 Book: Key Tracks 2034

Theme

On track.

What does it mean to you to be on the right path? How do you discern you are on the wrong track and, in fact, need to get back on the right track?

How do you navigate uncertain circumstances when you do not know what tomorrow will bring? How do you manage the stress of the unknown? Do you anticipate the best or worst case scenario?

What does "holding the key" mean to you? Is the "key" the figurative method for unlocking something which is closed to those who lack a "key"?

How do you know when you have those metaphorical "keys to success" to accomplish your goal? What if you do not know what your goal is? What if it is not yet defined, how do you clarify your goal?

Chapters Referenced

Book 20 Key Tracks 2034

1 CHAPTER 134: (2034) ROUGH-N-READY WAREHOUSE & TRACKS ZOR'S TRAIN: CAN TOPLINER'S KEY WORK ANYTHING? LONGFELLOW ARRIVES AT WAREHOUSE 4

2 CHAPTER 135: (2034) COURTLY COUNTY HUB TRAIN STATION: BACK AWAY FROM THE TRAIN STATION PICTURE WINDOW AS THEY CHATTER ABOUT EXPLOSION 26

3 CHAPTER 136: (2034) TRACKS: ZOR'S TRAIN: TOPLINER'S KEY FALLS AS UNCONSICOUS LONGFELLOW LETS TRAIN MOVE ON ITS OWN 35

4 CHAPTER 137: (2034) THE WATSON MOUNTAIN MANSION: OUTSIDE: GENE AND SAMMY SCRIBE GET CALLED ASIDE 44

5 CHAPTER 138: (2034) TRACKS: ZOR'S TRAIN: PICKS UP SPEED. ZOR MISSING 47

6 CHAPTER 139 (2034) TRACKS: ZOR'S TRAIN: THE TRAIN ANNOUNCEMENT 54

7 CHAPTER 140: (2030) TRACKS: ZOR'S TRAIN: DOGS AND LONGFELLOW 57

8 CHAPTER 141 (2034): TRACKS: ZOR'S TRAIN: CAN ZOR BE FOUND 60

Preparation for Group Structured Activities

Group leader will need: A virtual or physical place to write so audience can see all group notes; A way to interact with the audience; These activities can also be assigned as homework; or they can be performed with an interactive group.

Structured Activity 1

Prepare your own list to help you get "back on track" if you ever feel as if you are off track in life.

Write an action you can take for each item below:

1. State why you feel you are off track. What events are happening in your life, and what is your emotional response, which makes you feel things are out of sorts?

2. Admit if you have made a mistake. Admit if your mistake resulted in you feeling lonely, or as if you do not belong.

3. Be objective and realistic. List what is in your control, and what events transpired which were out of your control. How will you "let go" of the things you were not able to influence?

4. Remind yourself you are not the only one feeling miserable.

5. Avoid hiding in your figurative "cave". List ways you will reach out to other people in a friendly manner... even if you do not feel up to it.

6. Write down two times you felt happy and content in your life. Write down the elements in those two events which made you feel good.

7. Write a list (four or five examples) of positive memories, as follows:

    a) List the elements common to all these memories.
    b) Which remembered activity made you

happiest? Can you repeat that happy activity today?

c) Can you identify a group you might join which promotes that wholesome happy activity?

d) Describe the characteristics of a group where you feel you belong and are accepted.

e) If an identical gathering is no longer available, is there an alternative group which shares the characteristics that make you feel welcomed and comfortable?

8. When introduced to a new situation, you may encounter people you do not know. It might feel awkward at first, but you can put on a smile and assume the best. Make an effort. Take a deep breath. Remove the focus from yourself. Consider offering to help someone else. Offering assistance to others is beneficial for getting yourself re-centered.

9. Write one situation you are grateful for today. Even if it is a small thing. Next, write something you are thankful for each day for seven days. At the end of that brief time, see if your stress has been reduced, or even removed.

10. Look at, or interact with, a cute friendly pet. If you do not have one, consider visiting your local animal shelter and offering to volunteer.

11. Make a simple schedule and stick to it. Sometimes having a structure you can follow each day is helpful to get you back on track.

12. Make sure you get some exercise. Taking a brisk walk in the crisp fresh air can be beneficial.

Structured Activity 2

Partner with somebody you trust to start a conversation. Role play as if you are strangers.

Here are some rules to follow:

1) Ask questions, and listen for a response, before talking about yourself.

Use these **safe** topics.
   a) The weather.
   b) Gardening. For example, if you do not like to garden, ask them what their favorite fruit tree is.
   c) Neutral topics which are not prone to arousing emotions.
   d) Before the event, select topics which may be of interest to the types of people at the gathering and bring up interesting, non emotion-provoking facts to discuss. Have a set of questions ready to ask about these neutral topics.
   e) Focus on topics which are of interest to the other person. If you only discuss topics of interest to yourself, you risk being labeled a "bore" or a "boring person". To be interesting, you must be interested in the events and people around you.

2 Avoid the following topics:
   a) "Trigger topics" which may provoke argument.
   b) Avoid topics of medical procedures, general ills, personal blemishes or embarrassments, bodily functions, or anything which may occur in a bedroom, bathroom, toilet, or your personal closet.
   c) Avoid personal "inside jokes" as these will need to be explained to your audience.
   d) Avoid correcting others. Even if you

genuinely are the expert. do not say, "You are very wrong as it is this other way instead of the way you think it is, idiot."

e) If you are too witty, and the joke is cruel or cutting, then it may breed distrust in you. If somebody feels as if they are the brunt of your unkind jokes, they may laugh on the surface, yet be very wary and distrusting of future interactions with you.

f) Avoid blindly agreeing with everything the other speaker suggests. It will make you appear to be a "yes man" or "kiss up, kick down" personality. It is advisable you provide your perspective without being combative on the topic.

g) Do not ask personal questions about family. Allow the other person to raise such issues themselves.

h) Do not raise political or religious issues.

i) Do not ask "how much do you make or invest".

j) If you do not know if they are a sports fan, avoid speaking about a specific sports team as they may not have any thoughts on the topic. This applies to theater as well as other events.

k) Do not take it upon yourself to claim to be the expert in a topic, then commence instructing your immediate audience about how to do thus and such.

l) Do not over flatter your audience. Avoid saying things such as, "Why are you so handsome, or beautiful… it is distracting to me…"

    i. This is considered trite manipulation and should be avoided.

    ii. It is appropriate to give a genuine modest compliment.

    iii. For example, if you attended a conference and are introduced to the keynote speaker, you may say, "I really enjoyed the observation you made today in your lecture about X."

m) Avoid being tactless and rude. This means focusing on a specific characteristic of the person you are addressing.

    i. For example...

    ii. Do not say "you used to be so captivating years ago."

    iii. Do not say, "I really like your outfit. It is much more amusing than what is in fashion this year."

    iv. Do not say to a plump person, "Have you thought about going on a diet? Perhaps you should skip the cheesecake tonight."

    v. Do not say to a woman whose son has recently married, "Why do you think new wives despise their mothers-in-law?"

    vi. Do not say to a parent who may have lost a child to death, "Isn't it wonderful to have children around us during the holidays?"

    vii. Do not point to a person across the room and say, "That person is so ugly. I cannot believe they felt as if they could show up here wearing that. They are far too old, fat, poor, uneducated, ill-mannered to be doing XYZ."

    viii. Do not insult the other person, "You are such a half-witted moron."

2. Ask questions about hobbies you know they like.

3. Avoid interrupting the other person. Take a breath before you speak just in case they need to complete a sentence. If you are interrupted, instead of admonishing them, simply remain quiet until there is a natural pause allowing you to complete your

interrupted thought.

4. If you attempt humor, evaluate the reaction of your audience. If they are merely somber, do not laugh at your own joke. Avoid repeating the same story to an audience. Do not overly praise, nor condemn, nor gossip about, another person.

5. Before changing the subject, say, "That was interesting, but I was wondering about your opinion on [insert new topic here]".

6. If you are in a small group, try to look at each person and talk to each person. Involve everyone.

7. If somebody has something to brag about, let them. Do not try to out-do them with something you had worse or did better.

8. Do not share personal details about yourself.

    a) Do not ask the other person about any of their personal relationships. This means do not ask about children, loved ones, etc. Wait for them to bring it up before you discuss another person.

    b) Do not correct them on their grammar or anything else. Your job is to keep conversation flowing, not scolding.

Objective Achieved

Understand the nuances of polite conversation in a group setting.

Group Conversation

This is the proposed method for guiding a group in an open-ended discussion of a topic. The same topic may explore different aspects with different audiences. Start with a question to get the group interacting. Make sure all parties can participate and vocalize their opinions about characters and situations. Remember to thank the group for their participation and opinions.

After the host facilitates the following group discussion questions (see below), the host may ask attendees to complete an optional homework assignment by the next meeting.

1. What is the benefit of learning the art of conversation?

2. What makes a person interesting? What would make you interesting?

3. How do you convey to another person that you genuinely care about them? How would you convey you care to a coworker, classmate or acquaintance which you do not know very well? Why is it valuable to convey respect, consideration, and caring for your neighbor?

4. How would you answer the question, what is your favorite tree?

5. When evaluating goals in your life compared to goals in another person's life...

    a) Have you ever asked somebody about a goal

they want to accomplish?

b) Have you followed up by affirming that their goal is a worthy effort no matter how small or how large that goal is/was?

c) Have you asked where they started? Where did they want to go (goal-wise)?

d) What problems have they anticipated?

e) Do they have a plan to avoid or minimize those problems?

f) What is an overall plan of action to get them to their goal?

g) What can you do to help them achieve their goal and can you do this with a self-less heart instead of wondering what you can get out of it?

6. If you ever tried to accomplish something and did not quite make the goal, did you...

a) Learn something new? Learn something about what motivates you? Learn about the value of good character and determination? Learn something about what motivates others?

b) Did you become aware of something?

c) Did you learn how to do it better next time?

d) How did you measure your success or failure?

e) What new lists, plans, creative

brainstorming, priorities, decisions or agreements did you learn to make the next time?

7. If others were impacted by your "failure" of being "off track", how did you empathize with the impact it had on them?

    a) Did you acknowledge the pain or disappointment they felt?

    b) Did you explain why you made the choices you did to help them understand your logic and motives?

    c) Did you outline the facts you had available to you, and the elements which were hidden from you to explain the state of available information to help you make an informed decision?

    d) Did you ask them if they could tell you what they heard you just say to make sure they understand? Did you ask them if their feelings have changed now that they know your side of the story?

    e) Did you encourage them to have a different point of view or to ask you follow up questions?

    f) Did you take this opportunity to make a new agreement so you and the other party know what to expect from the other in the future?

    g) Did you consider this "failure" a success if you learned something from it?

Assignments (Optional)

Write down your ideas regarding open ended "safe" topics which will help to start a conversation with a person you have just been introduced to at a function.

Share your answers with others in your group.

End of Conversation Station for this Book 20.

21 Book: Hub 2031

Theme

Hubs and connections.

How do you know you have arrived at a point where you must definitely take a direction? A hub is a place where all vehicles arrive, and passengers can switch vehicles to continue their journey. Metaphorically, therefore, how many changes do you need to make to get to your destination?

One of the first train hubs in the United States. in Framingham, MA, dubbed itself the "hub of the universe." The slogan printed in handbills around the 1880's promoted, "If Not the Hub of the Universe -- the hub of a Territory containing 2,000,000 people within a radius of thirty miles". In the 1820s, many small railway companies were incorporated.

Even earlier than that, around 1720, a railroad became the mechanism of transport to assist in constructing a French fortress at Louisbourg, Nova Scotia, Canada.

At that time, this was a revolutionary manner of transportation. Today, different modes of transport are available to the average person. One thing transportation has in common, is that to get to your final destination, you may need to change direction or even modes of transport. This can be done at a hub.

Metaphorically speaking, are you probably at a point in your life where you may need to take a turn to get to your final destination?

Where will you go next? Are you now at a figurative cross-road?

Has one figurative door slammed shut? Do you see a figurative alternate path? An open window? Another door? How will you navigate your circumstances to know where to go next?

What helps you make a wise decision when you do not know the future, or to which destination this path will lead you?

Gone Book 26 Conversation Station- Book 21

Chapters Referenced

Book 21
Hub 2031

1 CHAPTER 142: (2034) TRACKS: ZOR'S TRAIN: ZOR'S DEAL 6

2 CHAPTER 143: (2034) COURTLY COUNTY HUB TRAIN STATION: SARAH PARADISE GIVES BACK THE BORROWED DRESS 13

3 CHAPTER 144: (2034) COURTLY COUNTY HUB TRAIN STATION: GENE AND SAMMY SCRIBE ARRIVE AT THE TRAIN STATION 16

4 CHAPTER 145: (2034) COURTLY COUNTY HUB TRAIN STATION: SARAH SEARCHES FOR GEORGIA 19

5 CHAPTER 146: (2034) COURTLY COUNTY HUB TRAIN STATION: SARAH REACHES FOR GEORGIA 23

6 CHAPTER 147: (2034) COURTLY COUNTY HUB TRAIN STATION: SARAH GRABS GEORGIA 27

7 CHAPTER 148: (2034) COURTLY COUNTY HUB TRAIN STATION: SAMMY SCRIBE AND GENE. TO THE RESCUE 30

8 CHAPTER 149: (2034) COURTLY COUNTY HUB TRAIN STATION: GEORGIA EXPLAINS. DOG BARKS 37

9 CHAPTER 150: (2034) COURTLY COUNTY HUB STATION. ANCORS OBSERVE TARGET 40

10 CHAPTER 151: (2034) COURTLY COUNTY HUB STATION. ANCORS ATTACK THE TRAIN SURVIVORS 46

11 CHAPTER 152: (2034) COURTLY COUNTY HUB TRAIN STATION: JUSTIN MEETS GENE 52

12 CHAPTER 153: (2034) COURTLY COUNTY HUB STATION: WARN LONGFELLOW TO STAY IN STATION WHILE ANCORS ATTACK 57

13 CHAPTER 154: (2034) COURTLY COUNTY HUB TRAIN STATION: GEORGIA EXPLAINS 63

Preparation for Group Structured Activities

Group leader will need: A virtual or physical place to write so audience can see the group notes. A way to interact with the audience. These activities can be assigned as homework or performed with an interactive group.

Structured Activity 1

Assume a 20 year old can walk three (3) miles per hour. Assume an elderly person can walk around two (2) miles per hour.

If 3 miles per hour translates to 264 feet per minute... and...

If 2 miles per hour translates to 176 feet per minute... and...

If escalators move at half the normal walking speed, 88 to 132 feet per minute, describe reasons why somebody would or should take an escalator instead of simply walking, when walking would be faster?

Discuss or list the advantages of using an escalator or conveyor belt?

Structured Activity 2

An escalator step is shaped a bit differently from a stair-case step. Escalator steps are taller, triangular in structure, and have a tread, which allows the steps to sink flat when needed and also to serve as traction so the bottoms of your shoes do not slip.

Both the escalator step and the stair step have the same purpose which is to provide a surface on which a person may place their foot and stand.

What other common object can you name which has the same purpose, yet is designed differently when stationary versus moving?

If moving people from point A to point B was the goal, discuss other transportation methods and what infrastructure is needed to allow these vehicles to have hubs of connections.

 1. eVTOL, or electric Vertical Take Off & Landing in a vertiport

 2. Helicopters which use a heliport

 3. Airplanes which use a airport

 4. Space shuttles which use a launch pad

 5. Horses which use stables and hitching posts

 6. Cars or other 4-wheeled vehicles which use parking lots

 7. Ships or boats which use docks

Discuss the purpose served by the elements in designs of a staircase and how it evolved into an escalator. How did the banister need to be redesigned as it moved from a staircase to a moving escalator, for example.

Write a need you see today, and write the type of "invention" which would fill that need. Even if that "invention" does not yet exist, what properties or characteristics of that invention would solve the problem, in your opinion.

Objective Achieved

Learn how to apply an invention's purpose to an actual need. Understand the the vehicle is one component, but the infrastructure needed to create a hub so this vehicle can be used for a population of people is also important to plan.

Group Conversation

This is the proposed method for guiding a group in an open ended discussion of a topic. The same topic may explore different aspects with different audiences. Start with a question to get the group interacting. Make sure all parties can participate and vocalize their opinions about characters and situations. Remember to thank the group for their participation and opinions.

After the host facilitates the following group discussion questions (see below), the host may ask attendees to complete an optional homework assignment by the next meeting.

1. What transportation do you use today, and why?

2. What would make you trust or distrust a mode of transportation?

3. The first patent for an escalator-like moving staircase powered by steam was granted in 1859. In 1895 a patent was granted for a design which leveraged elevator technology. This people-moving conveyor belt invention started as a ride at Coney-Island in New York, NY. Later, it was installed in a store where people were rewarded if they would take the escalator instead of a staircase. What type of transportation do you view as "new and novel" which later may become commonplace? s

4. In this story, the HUB station is more than a place to make a connection. What events transpired in this story and how did learning of those events make you feel?

Assignments (Optional):

Evaluate your local area. Identify a problem. If this problem were resolved, would it make life better for a group of people?

Complete the blanks in the following paragraph.

To make life better for _____, we need something to fix the problem of _____. The solution should have these characteristics or attributes: _____. This is what is needed to maintain the safety of the vehicle used to address the problem _____. This is what is needed to maintain the hub of connection this vehicle will use to make it available to the public _____.

Once you have documented your problem, and a high level description of a solution, get more detailed in describing your solution even if it does not yet exist.

End of Conversation Station for this Book 21.

22 Book: Camp 2034

Theme

Belong.

How do you know where you belong?

Do you feel as if you do not "fit in"?

The term "belong" was first used in the mid 1300s. It meant "to go along with" and some felt it was used to mean "be the property of" or "be a member of", which was used in the late 1300s. Some believe it is derived from Dutch "belangen" or German "belangen"

This is a term which refers to a place where you are accepted, respected, and valued. If you are in a particular place and wondering if others in the group view you favorably, then that very act of examination means you doubt they do. It will add to your stress and consume your energy. If you feel as if you are an outcast, or rejected from a group, then that is an even more stinging injury to your soul.

Think about what you can do to make others feel as if they belong.

Identify one of your your important values and decide why that value is important to you. Be interested in others, and actively engaged in social communication, by asking others what their important values are. Have you told somebody else that you support their positive skills? Are you able to articulate specifics so that your comment does not sound like an empty platitude?

But if your environment is hostile, then be alert to know when you should strategize to disassociate and transition to another group.

How can you craft an environment which is welcoming to yourself along with others who are also positive and supportive?

If you feel as if you do not belong, then you may experience stress. If you feel actively threatened, then you certainly will experience stress.

When your body and mind feel threatened, the hypothalamic-pituitary-adrenal axis (HPA) goes into action, releasing cortisol, a stress-hormone. When the brain surges with high levels of cortisol, distress signals are sent to the hippocampus, the part of your brain which learns, thinks, and remembers things.

Cortisol also impacts the cortex, the part of your brain which is used for high order cognitive abilities. To be organized and reliable, you may need your cortex. If your actions are impulsive, you disregard consequences, appear to be a "drifter", or crave chemical numbing agents, then stress may be interfering with signals getting to your sophisticated thinking skills, which you need for useful decision making, evaluating, deciding which rule to use when, brainstorming and creativity. All these are functions considered "higher order cognition".

So if you feel like you cannot absorb facts, or cannot remember...then this may be a reaction to stress. That stress may have been caused by you feeling rejected from a social group.

Chapters Referenced

Book 22 Camp 2034

1 CHAPTER 155: (2034) ANCOR ROAD: WAKE UP TO THE SMELL OF ATTACK 4

2 CHAPTER 156: (2034) ANCOR ROAD TO CAMPSITE: PIT STOP WITH ANCORS 11

3 CHAPTER 157: (2034) ANCOR CAMPSITE: WAKE UP, ANCOR...WAKIE, WAKIE 17

4 CHAPTER 158: (203x) ANCOR CAMPSITE: GOOD WORK RECRUITS, DUSTIN AND AUSTIN 22

5 CHAPTER 159: (2034) ANCOR CAMPSITE: CALL TO ACTION- DISPATCH THE RECRUITS 29

6 CHAPTER 160: (2034) AROMAX FOREST: RECRUITS FIND ANCORS ON FOOT 32

7 CHAPTER 161: (2030) ANCOR CAMPSITE: BJORN & OTTO AND WARREN GET AWAY 62

Preparation for Group Structured Activities

Group leader will need: A virtual or physical place to write so audience can see the group notes; A way to interact with the audience; These activities can be assigned as homework or performed with an interactive group.

Structured Activity 1

List the areas to which one could belong. Then highlight where you feel welcomed and where you do not. Do you think the actions, attitudes, and values of the people in these groups describe you and your values? Include the following:

1) Family
2) Friends
3) Social groups
4) School
5) Work
6) Community

Structured Activity 2

Take the list in Activity 1 and write down the ways you "connect" to the people in that group. What actions do they do which make you feel welcomed, valued, appreciated, and that you belong there?

What can you do in these groups which would make a new person feel as if they now belong?

Objective Achieved

Understand the power of belonging: When to leave an unhealthy situation; When to welcome others; What to do if you do not feel welcomed.

Group Conversation

This is the proposed method for guiding a group in open ended discussion of a topic. The same topic may explore different aspects with different audiences. Start with a question to get the group interacting.

Make sure all parties can participate and vocalize their opinions about characters and situations. Remember to thank the group for their participation and opinions.

After the host facilitates the following group discussion questions (see below), the host may ask attendees to complete an optional homework assignment by the next meeting.

1. Are you surrounded by forces or people who do not want you to succeed?

2. How might you manage that, and then move away from that harmful group and get to join a group of encouraging people who can help you on your journey to success?

3. Do you think a "temporary situation" can become permanent?

4. How can you stop the stagnation and keep moving forward on your journey?

5. Where and when will you "pitch camp" to rest, feel safe, and trust fellow campers at the campsite you have selected?

6. What can you do to foster or create an environment where you and others may feel welcomed, friendly, valued and appreciated.

7. If you are a new person entering a new group, what attitude should you have and what assumptions should you have about the members of the group?

Assignments (Optional)

How do you define "belonging"?

Do you think you need to connect to one person or a group of several people?

If you only need to connect to one person, can you identify who that person would be? Would this person believe in your abilities and encourage you when you are feeling glum, acting as a shield of protection from an attacking "rejection-monster".

If you need to connect with an entire group: 1)Document what that group is. 2)What values do they have which you admire or wish to adopt as your own?

What formula do you think would work for you to figure out attitudes you have and actions you can take to enter a new group and connect with people to start forming healthy supportive relationships?

What signs will you use to alert you that you are in a negative disruptive situation which is taking a mental toll on your health and that it is time to cut ties and leave that relationship?

End of Conversation Station for this Book 22.

23 Book: Plan 2034

Theme

Plan.

A plan of action may require a back up plan. Some believe a "back up plan" will prevent you from being bold enough to follow the original plan. Others counter that school of thought by saying if something outside of your control derails your first plan, having a back up plan allows you to quickly adjust, re-calibrate and keep moving forward.

Which school of thought do you believe in?

Or do you prefer to never plan, see how fate unfolds, and let things happen to you? How would you react if that passive path means somebody with corrupt intent has control over your life and your actions?

Would you willingly relinquish those freedoms to a bossy autocrat or would you defend your choice and freedoms by objectively evaluating the facts and developing a plan to keep you and those around you safe and free?

When do you forge forth? When do you grasp at passing wisps of an idea? When are you forcing a situation and when are you taking a foolish gamble with the resources entrusted to you?

Chapters Referenced

Book 23 Plan 2034

1 CHAPTER 162: (2034) COURTLY COUNTY HUB TRAIN STATION: MEET THE EX WATSON CONVERTS 4

2 CHAPTER 163: (2034) AROMAX TRAINSTATION: LONGFELLOW ARRIVES 10

3 CHAPTER 164: (2034) AROMAX FOREST. LONGFELLOW REJOINS THE TROOPS 15

4 CHAPTER 165: (2034) COURTLY COUNTY HUB TRAIN STATION: WHAT CAUSED THE EXPLOSION? 23

5 CHAPTER 166: (2034) ROAD: INFILTRATE 35

6 CHAPTER 167: (2034) HOMELESS SHELTER: PLANNING 48

7 CHAPTER 168: (2034) AROMAX BOARDROOM BUILDING: START THE AROMAX SNEAK ATTACK 55

8 CHAPTER 168 (2034) AROMAX BOARDROOM BUILDING: START THE AROMAX SNEAK ATTACK 68

Preparation for Group Structured Activities
Book 23

Group leader will need: A virtual or physical place to write so audience can see the group notes; A way to interact with the audience; These activities can be assigned as homework or performed with an interactive group.

Structured Activity 1

Think about all your items and put them into categories.

1. <u>*For clothing:*</u>

    a) What fits and what will you keep because you do look your best in it?

    b) What fits, but you will give away because you do not look your best in it?

    c) What other items will you give away or throw away?

    d) Can you set aside time to really pull everything out of your closet and drawers, clean out what you can give away, and then recognize your living area so only what makes you look and feel your best and fits you well remain in your wardrobe?

2. <u>*Books & papers:*</u>

    a) What do you need to reference regularly?

    b) What do you need to reference, but has an expiration date, after which you can give that away or throw it away? Do you have a place where you can put these things so you can dispatch them on a regular basis?

    c) What books do you want to keep because you just love them? Do you have a place for them?

    d) Do you have a place to file papers? Do you

have a way to match up your physical items with corresponding computer files of the same name?

3. <u>*Personal memory triggers*</u>:   You may need to go over these with a friend or family member to decide how to store them. (Photos or other memory triggers of happy times.)

4. How will you handle all the other things?

5. Document about how much time you think it will take for you to get organized.

Structured Activity 2

Think about your home and how you live. Draw your floor-plan. Assign a zone to each area of your home to indicate boundaries for activities. For example; Food preparation should be in the kitchen. This is the food zone. That means food should remain in the kitchen and not end up in your bedroom.

Objective Achieved

Plan your immediate environment. Your goal is to be organized. When you know you can always find something and you develop the discipline to always put it back where it belongs, you no longer waste time searching for that missing item. You reduce stress. You achieve more because you will know where everything is at all times. Your surroundings will be ordered, which means you can now focus your energy on creating great things.

Group Conversation

This is the proposed method for guiding a group in an open ended discussion of a topic. The same topic may explore different aspects with different audiences. Start with a question to get the group interacting. Make sure all parties can participate and vocalize their opinions about characters and situations. Remember to thank the group for their participation and opinions.

After the host facilitates the following group discussion questions, the host may ask attendees to complete an optional homework assignment by the next meeting.

1. Discuss, as a group, the challenges you face with organizing your personal space. What are tips you can give each other, or yourself, which will help you get organized?

2. Review this assignment as a complete class and see which items apply to you.

Assignments (Optional)

Pick an area in your home which you feel is disorganized and, with care, organize it.

1. Set aside a time-line with a clear start time and ending time. Realize you may *not* get everything done in that first block of time, but commit to planning for getting well-organized so you can better map out reaching your goal. You may have to set aside one day a week for a few weeks in a row. Stay focused on

dedicating that time slot to accomplishing the planned task. Celebrate when you do get it done.

2. Remember you will be grouping things to dispose of first, before you organize and arrange what remains. Set aside a pile, or bag, for "give away" and "throw away". Once you have those piled up, get rid of those bags appropriately. Then schedule some time to organize what you have remaining.

3. Make a plan and stick to it.

4. Identify what task is going to be the most challenging and tackle that one first.

5. Give each item a category. Then determine if those categories are grouped together properly.

6. Decide what to eliminate. What no longer fits into your every day life? What had been a gift from a loved one, but you, now, have no use for it so you are keeping it for sentimental reasons? Why are you keeping it? Are you afraid you may never get that kind of gift again in the future? Once you break up your excess into these categories, decide what you must truly keep and what you can donate to another person to make their life happy.

7. Give yourself a finite amount of time to execute the task. At the end of that time, take a rest and then set aside more time with a clear and definite stopping point. You do not want such an activity to drag on forever because then you will avoid it.

8. Zone your living area. What activity goes in which location? Stick to it. If food belongs in the kitchen, then it should stay in the kitchen. That means no food should be in your bedroom. If you need access to supplies on a regular basis, make sure those items are within reach. Think about how you live and zone your home to match your life.

9. Look at all of your clothes. You may have some things stored away for another season. You may have other things in closets and drawers.

   a) Pull all your clothes together and try them on to see what fits. Then determine if that item makes you look great and if you are comfortable wearing it. If you love it, keep it.

   b) Give everything else away. Next, move on to something like towels. Look at all the towels in your home. What do you have in the bathroom? What do you have in the kitchen? What do you have in storage? Are any of them getting old, have stains, holes, etc? Can you eliminate those from your home?

   c) Check each category left. Evaluate everything remaining to see if you really need all the remaining clutter around you, or if you can remove some more of it. Keep this up until you have completed all your categories.

   d) When it comes to personal items, you may wish to ask friends and family to help you sort through them and consider creative ways to store them and reference them in the future.

e) In your work space or office:

   i. identify what you need to reference for a short time,

   ii. identify what you need to reference until something happens, say a "quarterly report" you may need to complete.

   iii. identify what you want to keep forever.

   iv. Review the following list to place into the Daily pile, the Every so often pile, and the Forever piles.

   > Includes shopping receipts which may be in a book-bag, briefcase, purse, wallet, or handbag.

   v. Keep all important papers together in a neat file and label the file so you can reference it when you need to.

   vi. Review expiration dates and remove anything that has expired.

   vii. Group items which need action now or can be done later by adding to a "to do" list.

   viii. Schedule time to complete your "to do" list. Also schedule time to get organized by following the procedures in this list.

10. Find a place for everything. Make sure if you use something, you put it back in its place. Every object should belong in a specific place. Remember to put it back where it belongs. That way you won't lose

things.

11. Get a label maker and put labels on each item so that you can identify them again easily.

12. Set a schedule to weekly organize the following spaces:

    a) Space for "waiting on a response from somebody".

    b) Have a space for "topics I need to discuss with a specific person".

    c) Have a space for "Items I need to read, or actions which need to be taken" .

    d) Have space for "archived items I need to keep but have already been completed by me"

13. Now for your future: Get a planner. Schedule all the events identified in this planner along with contact information for those you need to meet and with whom to coordinate. Each day you will have tasks. Remember to prioritize them. Remember to categorize your tasks. Estimate time needed for completion of each task so you can see what may need to be scheduled for later.

    a) Calendar

    b) Contact list

    c) List of things I could not do today, but will do in the future list.

    d) Locations and directions to those locations

e) To Do List (prioritize, and estimate time to complete, this action item). Categories could be: Home, Personal, Work, School, Family, Hobby.

    i. Monthly actions could include Pay rent, pay other bills, create plans for X next month, file important papers, review desk for clutter and discard expired items, balance checkbook, plan menus for next month, back up electronic devices, replace filters.

    ii. Yearly actions could include: Visit doctor for annual check up; Schedule semi-annual dental cleaning; rotate tires on car; verify car maintenance is current; document goals for next year; clean out old computer files; learn X; etc.

f) List of goals. "In 6 months, I want to…"

g) Common lists (Grocery, shopping, entertainment you want to see, coupons/discounts with expiration dates, family trackers, pet trackers, gift ideas, wish list, daily journal, log your moods so you can see if your mood changes because of an event, or because you had too much to do that day). And remember to write up a Thankful List. This is a list of things you are thankful for. Jot down something new when you are inspired. Then, when you are feeling below average, you can read this list and lift your spirits.

h) Align your physical organization folders with your computer folders so everything has its place.

14. Remember that you should put away the things you are not working on when your day ends. Close it down. Clear off your desk. Be fresh the next day when you resume work. Sort and file your mail and make sure your items are organized. Clear off clutter daily or weekly.

The lesson learned is that it takes effort to set up a plan, but if you can maintain it, then it will be much easier to be organized. You will become more efficient and productive.

★★ ✦ ★★

End of Conversation Station for this Book 23.

24 Book: Finally 2035

Theme

Finally reaching a goal.

How do you feel when you have accomplished something? How do you feel when the tedious consistent effort you have expended results in a victory?

The word "satisfaction" was used in the early 1300s to refer to an act set forth by a church authority to atone for a sin. It is thought to derive from the 1100's Latin root which meant to satisfy a creditor to whom you owe a debt. The word denoted an "action of gratifying" also used around the late 1300s.

Have you considered if meeting a goal for you is paying off a debt? Or does meeting a goal to you involve gratification?

How would you determine if somebody was genuine or not? Are you "genuine"? What does that mean to you?

Some say trust is earned when you can demonstrate you are consistently reliable in presenting fact-based high-quality results. How do you define "trust", "quality" and how do you feel after you finally attain the truth after filtering through endless lies?

Chapters Referenced

Book 24 Finally 2035

1 CHAPTER 169: (2034) AROMAX BOARDROOM BUILDING: HEAT OF BOARDROOM TAKEOVER 3

2 CHAPTER 170: (2035) COURTLY CITY: LIBRARY: CHRISTMAS TRIP 26

3 CHAPTER 171: (2035) COURTLY CITY: TRAIN STATION: DECEMBER TRAIN TRIP FOR SARAH 31

4 CHAPTER 172: (2035) AROMAX: TRAIN STATION: AROMAX TRAIN STATION MEETING 46

5 CHAPTER 173: (2035) AROMAX TRAIN STATION: OUTSIDE: AROMAX CHRISTMAS 53

6 CHAPTER 174: (2035) AROMAX: GEORGIA HOME: AROMAX WHERE GEORGIA IS STAYING 62

7 CHAPTER 175: (2035) AROMAX CHURCH: CHRISTMAS EARLY EVENING -CHURCH WEDDING 71

8 CHAPTER 176: (2030) AROMAX: CHURCH: CEREMONIAL ENDING & HOPEFUL BEGINNINGS 91

Preparation for Group Structured Activities

Group leader will need: A virtual or physical place to write so audience can see the group notes; A way to interact with the audience; These activities can be assigned as homework; or performed with an interactive group.

Structured Activity 1

Write a paragraph answering the question "are where you are meant to be today, or not"? Why do you think this? Is this within your control or are there external factors outside of your control which halted your progress?

If there were external factors stopping you from attaining your goal, what can you do today to make progress or will you redefine your goal?

If you redefine your goal, clearly define it and write it down.

What steps can you take in the next month, week, and by tomorrow to start achieving your goal?

Structured Activity 2

Write a paragraph or two stating:

1. My definition of "success" is_____

2. The skills I need to attain this "success" are____

3. This is how my efforts to reach my goal are actually helping others:_____

4. After I reach my goal, this is how it will benefit me, and those around me.

Objective Achieved

Set goals, but make sure you are improving the lives of others when you focus on your own goal. If something blocked you from attaining your goal, how can you define a new strategy to achieve a different goal given your current situation?

Group Conversation

This is the proposed method for guiding a group in an open ended discussion of a topic. The same topic may explore different aspects with different audiences. Start with a question to get the group interacting. Make sure all parties can participate and vocalize their opinions about characters and situations. Remember to thank the group for their participation and opinions.

After the host facilitates the following group discussion questions (see below), the host may ask attendees to complete an optional homework assignment by the next meeting.

1. When you have satisfied an "urge", do you feel relieved or gratified?

2. In the back of Book 24, there is vocabulary from Book 21. Why do you think that it was important to understand the original word from which the Mattick names were created?

3. When you achieve a goal, how do you feel?

4. How did you act when you set a goal, but could not reach it?

5. Did you set a new goal or did you simply learn more skills or practice more so you could achieve your original goal?

6. How would you describe your journey to reach a goal, and your feeling of accomplishment, to another person unfamiliar with your journey?

7. Here is a passage from the book. Read it and share what it means to you. Why are Otto and Bjorn are discussing this?

"So, with the flowers, he can make fresh cyanide?" Bjorn asked, "Does he want to kill the guards he just knocked down?"

*Otto Mattick interjected, "Cyanide could kill a frog, but it would speed up a rabbit heart. If **glutathione** or **epinephrine** is added to the **perfusate**, then perhaps you could save the rabbit, otherwise, bunny heart would turn rock hard, killing the rabbit."*

"And that means?" Bjorn prompted.

"It means," Otto Mattick explained, "That if he can spray or paint the cyanide onto the suits of armor, it will kill the muscular functionality of the armor permanently. Then, all we have to do is extract each guard from the suit of armor. It won't hurt the guard, but it will fry the suit."

a) This is a general description of words used in the passage.

   i. **Glutathione**, *antioxidant found in most cells, can prevent damage to important cellular components caused by reactive oxygen species such as free radicals, peroxides, lipid peroxides, and heavy metals*

   ii. **Epinephrine** *can be another term used for another term for adrenaline. It is a hormone and neurotransmitter produced by the* *adrenal glands. Epinephrine has been used as a drug.*

iii. **Perfusate** *is a fluid used in perfusion.* **Perfusion** *describes the process of delivering something, say blood, via the circulatory system or the lymphatic system to deliver oxygen or nutrients to an organ or tissue.*

8. Read these definitions in Book 24 (see below). Next, read the lyrics (Next page is in Latin and the page after is in English in the next two pages). Discuss your interpretation of these lyrics. Have you heard it with music? At what occasion would you play this music?

Spem in Alium This is the Latin title for the musical composition by Thomas Tallis in 1570. It is translated to mean "Hope in Another". In this story, it was sung during the wedding by forty sopranos, altos, tenors, baritones and bass voices in practiced harmony.

Laudate Dominium was composed by Wolfgang Amadeus Mozart in Salzburg around 1780. It was also in 'Silversmith's Pearls of Wisdom', which was started in 1776 in the Firebrand series. The English translation of the Latin "Praise the Lord all nations; Praise Him all people."

Latin Laudate Dominium

Laudate Dominum omnes gentes
Laudate eum, omnes populi
Quoniam confirmata est
Super nos misericordia eius,
Et veritas Domini manet in aeternum.

Gloria Patri et Filio et Spiritui Sancto.
Sicut erat in principio, et nunc, et semper.
Et in saecula saeculorum.
Amen.

Gone Book 26 Conversation Station- Book 23

English Laudate Dominium

Praise the Lord, all nations;
Praise Him, all people.
For He has bestowed
His mercy upon us,
And the truth of the Lord endures forever.

Glory to the Father and to the Son and to the Holy Spirit,
as it was in the beginning, is now, and forever,
and for generations of generations.
Amen.

Assignments (Optional)

Define a new goal.

Define the skills needed to achieve that goal.

Document how your efforts will help others. How would it help which type of person?

What other resources do you need to attain this goal?

Can you set a date when you will start working on this goal. Can you estimate by what date you will plan to achieve this goal? What are the consequences if you do not achieve it?

End of Conversation Station for this Book 24.

25 Book: Longfellow's Journal 2028 to 2031

Theme

Longfellow's Journal, a personal journey.

In this book, Longfellow wrote his most private thoughts in a journal. These musings add extra nuanced understanding about his inner motivations during key points in the story of GONE.

Do you keep a journal?

If you do, do you find it useful to look at past pages to see how far you have come? Does reviewing a history of your own life encourage you when things get rough?

How do you record your personal journey?

Have you encountered a person who hogged all the credit for themselves, but placed blame on others?

Have you known somebody who demonstrated valor and nobility by acknowledging some actions which held them back, yet was still determined to move forward despite the odds?

How have you dealt with people who evidence their jealousy and vehemence, which translates into actions of sandbagging, disrupting and sabotaging your efforts.

How can you endure the attacks of others, yet make hard choices by moving on, not letting resentment or blame hold you down from achieving what you were meant to accomplish?

Chapters Referenced

Book 25
Longfellow's Journal
Year 2028 to 2031

1 CHAPTER LOG ENTRY: 2028 AROMAX POPULATION PROBLEM 2

2 CHAPTER LOG ENTRY: 2028 MEET THE TWINS 3

3 CHAPTER: LOG ENTRY: 2028 TWINS PRODUCTS ARE GARBAGE 5

4 CHAPTER: LOG ENTRY: 2028 DIPLO IN CHARGE OF GLEK LOGISTICS 7

5 CHAPTER:LOG ENTRY: 2028 GLEK HIJACKED 8

6 CHAPTER: LOG ENTRY: 2028 TWINS SORRY ABOUT DIPLO 9

7 CHAPTER: LOG ENTRY: 2028 DR. LOU POLE LINDEN LOVES THE TWINS 10

8 CHAPTER: LOG ENTRY: 2028 DR. LOU POLE LINDEN "LAB RAT" WHO WON'T LISTEN TO REASON 12

9 CHAPTER: LOG ENTRY: 2028 DIPLO MEETS WATSON AND SEEMS HAPPY 15

10 CHAPTER: LOG ENTRY: 2028 DIPLO MISSING 17

11 CHAPTER: LOG ENTRY: 2029 MUSEUM GALA. NEW ACQUISITION: TALLMAN DIARY 19

12 CHAPTER: LOG ENTRY: 2029 RESEARCHING OPTIONS WITH OTHER CORP CITIES 21

13 CHAPTER: LOG ENTRY: 2029 TURNED AWAY AT MUSEUM, WILL TRY AGAIN LATER 22

14 CHAPTER:LOG ENTRY: 2029 REACHED OUT TO PRIS' SISTER, QUEENIE COURTLY 23

15 CHAPTER: LOG ENTRY: 2029 DAY IN AROMAX TEST GARDEN 25

16 CHAPTER: LOG ENTRY: 2029 NEW PASSION FLOWER EXHIBIT AT MUSEUM OPENING SOON 26

17 CHAPTER: LOG ENTRY: 2029 PASSION FOR PASSIONFLOWERS AT THE MUSEUM 27

18 CHAPTER: LOG ENTRY: 2029 ATTENDED MUSEUM EXHIBIT ON PASSIONFLOWERS 29

19 CHAPTER: LOG ENTRY: 2029- JACK LOVED LONGFELLOW'S IDEA 32

20 CHAPTER: LOG ENTRY: 2029 BACK FROM COURLTY CITY AND HEADED TO MUSEUM 33

21 CHAPTER: LOG ENTRY: 2029 HEADED TO TEST GARDENS TO TELL PRIS: FAILED PROPOSAL 34

22 CHAPTER: LOG ENTRY: 2029 FEELING BETRAYED AND DISGUSTED WITH WORLD 49

23 CHAPTER: LOG ENTRY 2029: LOU POLE LINDEN IS LONGFELLOW'S BOSS 50

24 CHAPTER: LOG ENTRY: 2029: TWO DAYS AFTER LOU POLE LINDEN'S PROMOTION 51

25 CHAPTER: LOG ENTRY 2029: DAY OF VOTE 53

26 CHAPTER: LOG ENTRY 2029: A WEEK AFTER THE VOTE 56

27 CHAPTER: LOG ENTRY: 2029 VISIT TO PRIS' OFFICE 57

28 CHAPTER: LOG ENTRY: 2029 PRIS GOOD BYE 58
30 CHAPTER: LOG ENTRY: 2030 SETTLING AT WINERY 65

31 CHAPTER: LOG ENTRY: 2031 MORE RECRUITS ARRIVING. EXHAUSTE 66

32 CHAPTER: LOG ENTRY: 2031 TRAINING ON ISLANDS IN "NECKLACE OF NETHERLANDS 67

33 CHAPTER: LOG ENTRY: 2031 "WHERE ARE YOU...NOT HOW ARE YOU... 69

34 CHAPTER: LOG ENTRY: 2031 HORSE BACK RIDING SKILLS IMPROVING AMONG RECRUITS 70

35 CHAPTER: LOG ENTRY: 2031 LESSON IN CHARM 71

36 CHAPTER: LOG ENTRY: 2031 HORSE LESSONS 73

37 CHAPTER: LOG ENTRY 2031   DAN SER 75

38 CHAPTER: LOG ENTRY: 2031 IN VLIELAND FOREST 76

39 CHAPTER: LOG ENTRY: 2031 BARRIER PREVENTS US FROM COMMUNICATING 77

40 CHAPTER:LOG ENTRY: 2031 MEMORIES EVOKED BY THE RED LIGHTHOUSE... 79

Preparation for Group Structured Activities

Group leader will need: A virtual or physical place to write so audience can see the group notes; A way to interact with the audience; These activities can be assigned as homework; or performed with an interactive group.

Structured Activity 1
Decide what would be the best journal format for you. Is it a paper book? Is it an audio recording? Is it a computer file? Is it talking to a close confidant?

Dedicate the right format for you and decide to keep a journal.

Decide what you want to track in your journal. Some people track moods, or weight, or the weather for each day. Others track when something good happens to them. You may also track answers to your prayers. You might decide to simply document the events of the day.

Select one thing you want to track so that you can correlate that one thing with how you feel, how your day and week and year are going.

Structured Activity 2
Start a thankful gratitude list. What can you appreciate in your life today? At the end of each month, summarize what you are grateful for the most.

Whenever you feel great, or you feel as if you have

had an answer to prayers, write down what you are thankful for.

This is your personal list which will grow over time. When you have a bad day or are doubtful about the future, refer to this list as a way to get yourself focused on the positive.

If you witness people in your life who demonstrate poor leadership, what actions can you take to improve the situation. Could you set an example by behaving better? Could you study the area which needs to be lead to really understand the challenges of leading and gain appreciation for the role? Could you discuss the matter with others under their leadership to see if your perspective aligns with theirs? How could you make life better for you, your leader and others who are being led and still comport yourself with integrity?

Consider these passages. How would you apply these to your situation:

...continue to think about the things that are good and worthy of praise. Think about the things that are true and honorable and right and pure and beautiful and respected.

Philippians 4:8 International Children's Bible

I repeat, be strong and brave! Do not be afraid and do not panic, for I, the Lord your God, am with you in all you do."

Joshua 1:9 New English Translation

He (God) restores my strength. He leads me down the right paths for the sake of his reputation.

Psalm 23:3 New English Translation.

Objective Achieved

Starting a personal journal so you can learn from your own history.

Group Conversation

This is the proposed method for guiding a group in an open ended discussion of a topic. The same topic may explore different aspects with different audiences.

Start with a question to get the group conversation started. Encourage interactions which are wholesome and positive.

Make sure all parties can participate and vocalize their opinions about characters and situations. Be a moderator and make sure nobody is insulted or put down for their point of view.

Remember to thank the group for their participation and opinions.

This is the final installment of the Conversation Station. Thank the group for their valuable contributions throughout this series.

1. What could future generations learn from your life?

2. How did you handle disappointment, trauma, failure?

3. Were you gracious with success, achievements and did your efforts positively impact the lives of others?

4. What can you do to make the lives of those around you better?

5. What have you learned from Longfellow's journal which you can apply in your own life?

6. Did reading Longfellow's journal give you a different perspective on the events which transpired in the GONE series?

7. What are the top (one, two or three) lessons you learned?

8. How do you think Longfellow's or the Mattick's life would have been if the Twins had not been around to change the balance of power? How would the people have fared?

9. At the end of the journal entries is a blank lined page inside Book 25. Here you can write how Longfellow inspired you. Does reading the journal inspire you to act or change the way you see things? Does it motivate you to do something? Write down the lessons you learned from reading his entries.

Assignments (Optional)

No assignments.

Have fun and read another book or start your own journal.

Ponder the poem written by Henry Van Dyke, (1852 to 1933).

Life

Let me but live my life from year to year,
With forward face and unreluctant soul;
Not hurrying to, nor turning from, the goal;

Not mourning for the things that disappear
In the dim past, nor holding back in fear
From what the future veils; but with a whole
And happy heart, that pays its toll
To Youth and Age, and travels on with cheer.

So let the way wind up the hill or down,
O'er rough or smooth, the journey will be joy:
Still seeking what I sought when but a boy,
New friendship, high adventure, and a crown,
My heart will keep the courage of the quest,
And hope the road's last turn will be the best.

End of Conversation Station for this Book 25.

26 Characters

Austin: This dog rustled up what needed tracking as Jack Russel Terrier. Jack Russel Terrier is the dog of Longfellow.

Bjorn Esterday: Reporter at the Daily Memo in Courtly City with a mistaken identity, a reluctant resident at Brio who tries to escape to get back home to Courtly City.

Bjorn Esterday: Reporter at the Daily Memo in Courtly City and with, a mistaken identity, now a resident at Brio.

Charlie Horse: The victim. Otto Mattick is accused of killing Mr. Horse

Dan Ser : A former resident of AromaX, now lives in Austria. He is a very good dancer and a polished gentleman who mingles with the upper classes easily. is a former resident of AromaX and friend of Longfellow. Dan Ser lives in Vienna. He is very refined and knowledgeable. He is a friend of both Longfellow and Warren Piece. All former AromaX residents.

Dr. Lou Pole Linden: Research assistant to Otto Mattick in the AromaX labs. He wants to create MagSols with Female1, Male 1 and Male2. He hates the bully authoritarian tactics of the Twins but he also lusts for power himself and fantasizes about replacing the Twins, yet he cowers at their threats.

Dustin, Austin, Tustin and Justin, the dogs of Longfellow Dustin, Tustin, Austin and Justin: Dogs cared for by Longfellow and Warren Piece. Dustin is a black Labrador retriever. Tustin is a white poodle. Justin is a Belgium Malinois. Austin is a Jack Russel Terrier.

Dustin: Labrador dog of Longfellow. black Labrador dog- dark like dust.

Earthie: This is the slang term used by the AnCors, Anti Corporatists, to reference a member of the Earth Farmer community in a derogatory manner.

Earth Farmer Preacher: Street preacher in Rough-N-Ready

Earth Farmer: society of peaceful low-technology people who made an agreement with Jack Courtly to farm and provide food to the citizens of Courtly City.

Elder James: Built homeless shelters, lives at the Widow's monastery cloister run by nuns. Elder James built a village in the story EDGES and now he is in GONE building another village to house the homeless of AromaX.

Female 1: Test Subject in the AromaX lab run by Dr. Linden and funded by the Twins

Georgia Peach: Fellow teacher at Sarah Paradise's school.

Guard Gene or Ivan Emillio Gene is an SP from Courtly City. As a Courtly City Soldier Police (SP) officer, he volunteers to build the shelter in AromaX. Guard Gene, has a strong sense of morals.

He has worked on the Courtly family train, in the jails, and one day he strives to become Detective Gene. Guard Gene Ivan Emillio Gene first appeared in EDGES as one of the guards assigned to protect the Courtly family on the Courtly train, which was attacked.

He appears in GONE volunteering to build a shelter for the citizens of AromaX. AromaX had experienced economic downfall after the Mattick family was unseated from power and replaced by a corrupt aggressive authoritarian government, which took the funding intended for the people. He is first referenced as Guard Gene, then later after a long over-due promotion, he is referenced as Detective Gene.

Jane Hargreaves: This is the maiden name of Sarah Paradise's mother. Sarah was informed her mother was named after a woman who lived in the 1770's (in the FIREBRAND series). To learn more about Sarah's ancestor from the 18th century please read about the adventures of Jane Hargreaves in the Firebrand series.

Justin: Belgium Malinois. Belgium Malinois dog of Longfellow

Longfellow: partners with Warren -Former resident of AromaX, now resides here and training recruits and working at a winery in the Netherlands where he sought refuge from the Twins take-over of AromaX.

He is the descendant of TallMan and friend of Warren Piece.

He runs the recruits, who became refugees from AromaX after the Twins took over. Descendant of TallMan (see Firebrand Series) and avid canine enthusiast. Friend of Warren Piece. Former AromaX resident who fled to a remote island to train other AromaX refugees so that he may unseat the Twins from power and reclaim his position in AromaX.

Leads a group of AromaX refugees which he calls recruits.

Originally from AromaX, he and companion Warren Piece fled AromaX when the Twins took control. Longfellow lives in a remote place near the Netherlands.

His ancestor is TallMan. Still longs for Pris Mattick when he was back in AromaX. He keeps a journal.

He reads a book created by Silversmith of wisdom from the 1770's FIREBRAND series. This is where he yearns to learn more of his ancestor, TallMan.

Male1: Test Subject in the AromaX lab run by Dr. Linden and funded by the Twins

Male2: Test Subject in the AromaX lab, but first to undergo Dr. Linden's NanoNevel procedure

Mattick: The Mattick family is an elite class in the city of AromaX.

Mrs. Libris: is the librarian in the last Courtly City library who only has her job because of an endowment which provided funds to keep the library funded for a century.

She manages the hard copies of documents. Most citizens are unaware of the library. Sarah Paradise has a heart for knowledge and learning and has made friends with Mrs. Libris.

Otto Mattick: Research assistant at the AromaX lab. One of the displaced ruling siblings of AromaX. He had to step away from ruling the city when the Twins took over.

The Mattick family dispersed and hid in other locations because they feared the ruthless authoritarian power of the Twins. Some Matticks accepted the abusive leadership at the cost of their integrity. Some tried to tolerate the rule of the Twins and others ran away or were mysteriously eliminated, never to be heard from again.

Otto remained determined to make things work, but then found himself trapped in a different way, falsely accused where running was the only way to save his life.

He faced overwhelming odds, yet never gave up. The Mattick family is recognized as an elite class in the city of AromaX.

Pat Seeds: Garden-keeper in Brio. Befriended Bjorn Esterday, yet always called Bjorn by another name while Bjorn was accused in trial for the entertainment of the other residents, but with drastic life/death consequences if he were convicted for a crime he never committed. Pat's job was to keep an eye on Bjorn during his anticipated short life in Brio.

Pip: Son of Skipper Courtly. Skipper called him "Pip" because it rhymed with "Skip", a shortened version of Skipper's own name.

Skipper also used this name because Skipper, being the risk taking gambler, would "roll the dice" and Skipper would call the dots on the dice a "pip". In 1797, "pip" was a term used to describe a seed in an apple or orange. Once, Skipper asked a man if he was British and he replied with the phrase *"Pips, core, the lot"* Which Skipper understood to mean that the man considered himself to be fully British, as if he were an apple. He was a full apple to the core, including the seeds and everything.

In other words, he was fully British to the very center or core of his being. Likewise, since Skipper is fixated on the pleasures money can buy, Skipper recalled his financial advisor explaining that a "pip" is a standard unit of measure being the smallest amount by which a currency quote can change.

It is usually $0.0001 for U.S.-dollar related currency pairs, which is more commonly referred to as 1/100th of 1%, or one basis point.

This standardized size helps to protect investors from huge losses."*percentage in point*" or "p*rice interest point,*" a tiny measure of the change in a currency pair in the **forex market**.

Most currency pairs are quoted to the fourth decimal place. A pip represents the last—and thus smallest—of those four numbers.

the word *Forex* is a concatenation, or a way of putting two words together. In this case, the term *Forex* puts together the words: **"foreign"** and **"exchange"**.

It is the largest financial market in the world, comprised of a variety of financial institutions, including banks, corporations, investors, and more.

PSL: Personal Security Lead, or bodyguard, employed by Watson and works at the Mountain Mansion.

Sammy Scribe: This is Bjorn Esterday's Editor in Chief or Boss at the Courtly City Daily

Memo. He found Sarah Paradise's information for Bjorn to lure him to cover a Watson motivational seminar in Courtly City.

Editor Sammy Scribe: Editor of the Courtly City newspaper, "The Daily Memo". He is referred to as "Editor" by the SPs who are trained to replace the Mr. and the Mrs. when addressing the citizens with their occupational title. Only the SPs (Soldier Police) can see the title of each citizen on the inside of their visors. The occupation informs the SP about the role the citizen should hold and if they have the permissions to conduct the activity they are currently undertaking when the SP decides to conduct a surprise inspection.

Sarah Paradise: Teacher in Courtly City. Met Bjorn Esterday in EDGES series. Became friends with fellow teacher, Georgia Peach.

Silversmith: This is a reference to a character in the Firebrand series. Silversmith authored "Silversmith's Pearls of Wisdom"

Slash: This AnCor has worked with Percy Snatcher, an AnCor leader. Slash has orchestrated attacks in Courtly City. Slash has done business with Topliner.

TallMan: This ancestor of Longfellow lived in the 1770s. He was a medicine man or doctor.

Topliner: The relative (nephew) of Otto Mattick

Tres: Works with Watson

Tustin: toffee nosed intelligent poodle, White poodle dog of Longfellow

Twins: These are a pair of powerful people who have stripped corporate cities like AromaX of their resources to rule them in a dictatorship. They plan to use MagSols to conquer more corporate cities.

The backstory of Courtly City is that it used to be an American-style democracy, however a couple of belligerent or hostile people lied to convince the population to place them in charge.

Once the Twins obtained power over the people, they spread lies to retain that power, seize more land and wealth, and spread negative propaganda about the former or rival leaders. These lies proved to be effective and prevented other - often better and more qualified leaders - to access the corporate throne. Those placed into influential positions were graded on how loyal they would be to the Twins. If they were willing to sacrifice their own reputation and knowingly lie to back up the false stories of the Twins, then they were rewarded with stolen goods and positions of influence even if they were not qualified for that position. This resulted in a mass population which suffered, and although skilled were not allowed to use those skills to benefit society.

Virginia Hamm: is an administrator who gives Sarah Paradise assignments.

Warren Piece: helps run the winery and is friends with Longfellow. He also works with the refugee recruits from AromaX and partners with Longfellow.

Warren is a former resident of AromaX, who now resides at the camp and helps Longfellow train the refugee-recruits. He also runs the local winery to help make money to continue training the AromaX refugees. He is a friend and confidant of Longfellow. He also trains the dogs and manages the vineyard. When assigned to a mission as a companion to Bjorn Esterday, Warren traveled to Rough-N-Ready.

Watson: Charismatic motivational speaker and has a working relationship with Zor of Brio.

Zor: Chief prosecutor of Brio, manager of Watson's worlds and has manages Watson's warehouse "farm" assets in Rough-N-Ready, where the rules are loose. Devoted to Watson's cons, Zor was in charge of Brio, and the pod farm in Rough-N-Ready where Watson's clients reside.

Meet the Mattick Family.

Pris Mattick, who was named because she was a burst of light and colorful rainbows, as found with a prism.

Pris fled when the Twins captured AromaX and assumed the identity of a brassy school teacher named **Georgia Peach.** Longfellow was in love with Pris, but was unable to act on his feelings until he was able to prove his devotion to objective integrity, honor, and strength with truth.

By staying true to his values, he also proved he supported AromaX under the leadership of the Mattick family. Pris vanished.

Gone into thin air.

Georgia Peach resurfaced with a plan which contributed to an overall plan of getting rid of the Twins.

Pris was the one who encouraged Longfellow to search for his roots in TallMan's artifacts, which she procured for him at the AromaX museum before the Twins shut down access to all AromaX cultural sites.

Kinem Mattick was nicknamed **Queenie** as a young girl. She met Jack, the youngest brother of the Courtly family and fell in love.

They were married and Queenie moved to Courtly City, but always brought with her the flare for fashion and style which were the hallmarks of AromaX. Kinem - or **Queenie Courtly** - always wanted to set the example for her child, Ace, to be actively modeling kindness and considerations of others.

Otto Mattick, was was named because he had to keep going automatically without any support nor intervention. Otto knew he had to disappear to avoid destruction from the Twins.

He swapped identities with an unknowing stranger. Little did Otto know this stranger was a Daily Memo reporter named Bjorn Esterday.

Little did Bjorn know that his own quest to get home opened up doors of enduring life changing love and friendship.

Only later did Bjorn realize he played a part in righting a wrong and helping the Mattick family reclaim AromaX.

Diplo Mattick, who assumed the Avatar of Pat Seeds in the underwater world of Brio. Diplo was the mother of Topliner.

She was always so careful to craft a diplomatic settlement between others that she began to neglect herself and then sought escape.

Her searching for something peaceful led her into Watson's and Zor's net of deceit She fell victim to the stories, yet realized she needed to break free.

In her pursuit to shed the shell of **Pat Seeds**,

Diplo also freed all the others in worlds seeking escape from an unbearable life.

After being in stasis in Zor's warehouse in Watson's Pod Farm, Diplo's muscles atrophied and she had to learn to move again in the real world.

With gentle patience, the well mannered Dan Ser left Vienna and returned to AromaX where a close friendship started to bud and could possibly blossom into a romance.

Topliner likes Dan Ser's positive effect on his mother, Diplo, so **Dan Ser** is a welcomed member of the family...should things develop along a more permanent alliance.

Meaning of the Mattick Names

From-Book 21

This vocabulary is inserted here to provide insight to the meaning behind the Mattick Family Names.

Prismatic Something which has the form of a prism, showing a spectrum of colored light. It can reference something which acts as one. Different colored light is not visible until a prism reveals all the separate elements which, when joined, form one bright light.

Used around 1709, meaning "of or pertaining to a prism". The term *prismatical* has been in use since the 1650s.

Diplomatic A way of causing good relations and avoiding bad feelings between parties. Modern meaning could be described as tactful, polite and skilled in win-win negotiations. Diplomacy is used to align governments of different countries. Around 1711 this term was used to relate to official documents and is thought to be from the Latin term *diplomaticus*. There was a collection of important public papers, some of which addressed international affairs. This collection of papers was called the *Codex Juris Gentium Diplomaticus* (1695)

Automatic Something which works by itself with no direct human control. Actions which are automatic are done without thought. .

Used around 1812 to mean moving or acting on its own. The term *automatical* has been in use since the 1580s. The term *automatous* has been in use since the 1640s. It suggests a form of automaton, which could be defined as a machine that performs a function according to a predetermined set of coded instructions in an automatic manner. Some say it is a machine designed to mimic human motion.

Kinematic The study of engineering mechanics focusing on the motion of an object without any reference to the forces which may trigger the motion. The branch of mechanics focuses on how an object moves and not why it is moving in the first place.

Used around 1840 to mean the science of motion. The term *Cinematic* was considered a variant of Kinematic and first used around 1883, but *cinematic* later became an adjective meaning pertaining to moving pictures or the cinema around 1914.

27 Locations

Alkamaar cheese market is where Warren Piece used to buy his cheese. ☐ Alkamaar cheese market had a cheese scale from the year 1365. On the 17th of June in the year 1593, the Alkmaar Cheese Carriers' Guild was established. This area is well known for its cheese.

AromaX: City of fragrance & fashion.

Brandaris lighthouse Part of the training course of the AromaX recruits, but Longfellow sometimes visited here to be alone.

Brio: Underwater village where Bjorn Esterday was given another name and was tried in a court for a crime he had not committed. Bjorn met Pat Seeds here.

Campsite: This is where the AnCors live.

Cologne: City in Germany where Cologne was first invented. Warren Piece went here.

Courtly City: City of solar & other technical products. Bjorn Esterday and Sarah Paradise live here.

Courtly County Hub Train Station: This is the train station stop where Georgia and Sarah find themselves midway between Courtly City and Watson's Mountain Mansion. This is a train station between the Watson Mountain Mansion and Courtly City. A mid-way train station between Courtly City and the Watson Mountain Mansion. Georgia may have crash landed near here.

Ecomare: Location where seals would gather near where Longfellow lived on the islands.

Island this is where Longfellow and Warren Piece protect recruits and AromaX refugees.

Keukenhof: A formal garden.

Maastrich winery/ vineyard: This is the winery/ vineyard managed by Longfellow to earn money to maintain the compound. Maastricht a place in the Netherlands where Longfellow has a winery. This is where the making of wine takes place. The business funds Longfellow and Warren Piece's effort to take in AromaX refugees and train them to one day take back AromaX from the Twins. Where Longfellow and Warren Piece made wine to sell and support the costs of running the compound, which shelters the recruits or refugees from AromaX.

Mayfounder Foundation. An organization favored the the current ruler of Courtly City, Skipper Courtly. If it was discovered this foundation was developing weapons, then that would violate a treaty between AromaX and Courtly City. This is a sham charity which has connections to Courtly City and Skipper Courtly, first seen in the series EDGES. The front promoted ecology conservation, while Skipper used it to make a profit on dumping toxic chemicals among other dubious activities.

Nes Ameland: A location where the recruits of AromaX took horseback riding lessons and learned about the long-maned Frisian horse breed. .

Nuremberg: City in Germany. Warren Piece went here on a mission.

Today, Nuremberg contains historic landmarks, like the imperial castle and the walled Old Town. The location of the city made it an important commercial hub from the Middle Ages. During WWII, the American's were victorious against the Nazis in the Battle of Nuremberg (1945). Nuremberg was in the center of the Nazi regime. To lose the city to the Americans took a heavy toll on already low German morale.

Later after WWII, The first international war crimes tribunal in history was held here. These trials revealed the wrongs inflicted by the German Nazis. Prominent Nazis were held accountable for their crimes. Modern society wanted to learn from the past and avoid a recurrence of such events.

Opera House: This is an historic formal building in which a formal dance takes place. In this story, it is located in Austria.

Rough-N-Ready: A town loosely governed by rules. This is where people go to conduct questionable business with no questions asked. AnCors operate here. Otto Mattick and Topliner perform at the theater here. a location where Otto Mattick and his nephew Topliner perform at the theater under different names. a place which rarely enforces laws so the AnCors thrive here and conduct business. The location where the AnCors can conduct business without fear of SP interaction.

The theater where Otto Mattick's nephew Topliner performs is here. This is a remote location loosely governed by laws where the AnCors can conduct business easily. This is where Longfellow, Warren Piece and some of his recruits may encounter a Mattick.

Otto Mattick and nephew Topliner perform

at the theater in Rough-N-Ready. They Topliner had taken on the name of Bjorn Esterday as a stage name. Zor, manager of Brio, may have a pod farm hidden away in Rough-N-Ready. This pod farm is used for all the worlds Watson manages, including Brio.

Schiermonnikoog - a location where Warren likes to procure his groceries- This island is in a province of **Friesland**, where long-maned horses are bred. It is situated between the islands of Ameland and **Rottumerplaat**. a tiny island where Longfellow and Warren visit. Originally a West Frisian Island of the Netherlands.

Terschelling marshes: Another location on the Island where recruits conduct exercises. AromaX recruit training area on the islands used by Longfellow and Warren Piece.

Texel sand dunes: Location on the small Island in the Netherlands near the Longfellow AromaX recruit training. This is where recruits conduct exercises A place with sand dunes which was useful for training the recruits. Longfellow had waited for the recruits at the dune of **Vuurboetsduin**, the second largest dune on the island. Here, he recalled his lost love with sweet memories from his days living in AromaX. Here, he wondered if he would ever find love like that, again.

Village: This is the shelter that Elder James planned. Guard Gene of Courtly City also helped to build this with other SPs. This is where Female1, Male1, and Male2 hope to live.

Vlieland forests: An additional location on the Island where recruits conduct exercises. Densely forested area used for training the recruits. This is where Longfellow and his team reside somewhere similar to the Netherlands

Watson Mountain Mansion: Sarah Paradise and Georgia Peach attend a lavish party here. Sarah Paradise and Georgia Peach attended a large party hosted here and where the PSL used Sarah's deductive reasoning to find a body. The location where a party was hosted. Both Georgia Peach and Sarah Paradise attended. The PSL asked Sarah's help on an investigation here. This is the home of the Motivational Speaker .He hosts a lavish party here. Watson's Home which was the location of a lavish party which Georgia and Sarah attended. This is where the lavish party occurs. The Echo is used to combine images of those dancing in another country to appear to dance as holograms at the Mountain Mansion

Zor's Train: This train is dedicated to the Watson business. One stop is in Rough-N-Ready. ★

28 Vocabulary (Alphabetized)

The fictional story of GONE had a vocabulary section at the end of each book. This section compiles and alphabetizes all books into one list. The term and definition is found in the left column, The right columns will mention the first time the term was used. In the definition, it will explain if this is a term unique to this world of Courtly City and AromaX or if it is a word you can find in the dictionary. In some cases, the English word may have a different meaning in the world of AromaX and Courtly City.

Alphabetized Vocabulary	First Found in the Vocabulary Section of this Book

A

88-2 (*Citrus reticulata Blanco*) this is an experimental variety of mandarin oranges. It has been grown in the University of California Riverside Experimental Citrus groves under the auspices of the College of Natural and Agricultural Sciences. 88-2 (*Citrus reticulata Blanco*) This is an experimental variety of mandarin oranges. It has been grown in the University of California Riverside Experimental Citrus groves under the auspices of the College of Natural and Agricultural Sciences.
Some have nicknamed this variety "Supernova" (CRC 3991, PI 539542, VI 501).

The ID is referenced in this story to illustrate how dedicated the character Pat Seeds is to her agricultural efforts. USDA 88-2 is a cross between Lee and Nova mandarins. It was developed at the United States Department of Agriculture Station in Orlando, Florida. Received as budwood

Book 09 Strawberry EarthShake 2032-2033

from the Florida A.H. Whitmore Foundation Farm, Leesburg, 1988.

Originally, in 1966, Jack Hearn, a U.S. Department of Agriculture citrus breeder, crossed Lee and Nova mandarins to understand pollination needs.

The result of these efforts was the production of a flavorful seedless variety he named 6-13-44. But, the tree did not bear fruit.

In 1988, he sent the sample to UCR hoping it would fare better in the Southern California climate.
It did, and the first commercial grower to plant it in 2010 was LoBue Citrus with a grove in Lindsay, southeast of Fresno.

Other premium varieties such as a large, easy to peel mandarin was named "Sumo" brought in by Sunkist Japan for Stark Bros. in 1998. Control then passed to a group led by Suntreat, which was bought by Agricultural Capital; they also own the registered trademark for Sumo Citrus®.

Some have surmised that this could be derived from a hybrid placed between Chung Gyun mandarins and Ponkan which are grown in Japan and Korea, or a Brazilian strain of 'Shiranui' called Guilietta.

There is a variety grown in the UCR experimental gardens which may be close to the Sumo: "Shiranui mandarin" (CRC 4249, VI 860) which is a Hybrid of 'Kiyomi' tangor (Citrus unshiu Marc. Crossed with Citrus sinensis Osb.) and 'Ponkan' (Citrus reticulata Bla.)"

Another premium flavorful variety is "DaisySL" (Citrus reticulata Blanco RUTACEAE), a cross between C reticulata 'Fortune' mandarin and C reticulata 'Fremont' mandarin). DaisySL was officially released by the University of California, Riverside, in June 2009.

Abaddon: a place of destruction. Book 16 Investigate 2034 This is considered an underworld location where lost souls who led morally corrupt lives are sent after they have died. It is a Christian belief that requesting forgiveness for sins and then changing your behavior and asking for God's grace and the strength to follow a godly lifestyle can save your soul from ending up in this place.

ACA- Anti-Corporate Activity. Usually applies to the AnCors. The ACA is sounded publicly by the SPs when their sensors pick up the presence of the AnCors. When an ACA alert is in progress, no wheeled vehicles are permitted on the pathways. This is to allow the SPs on horseback to chase the offender.

For citizens, the only mode of transportation available to them on the streets during an ACA is anything without a wheel.

The permitted vehicles include trains, horses, or any other mode of transportation not normally used on the street. Since the AnCors use older gasoline-powered cars and trucks, the SPs know that if those are on the road, then there are probably AnCors operating those vehicles. They become an easy target for the SPs.

The ACA was announced to the citizens when an AnCor, or Anti Corporatist plot may threaten the citizens. At that point, they were asked to halt all wheeled vehicles to allow the Soldier Police (SP) employed by the corporation, sufficient road to chase the offending AnCors. These alerts were used in Courtly City to

Book 01 Bubble Year 2030,

Book 02 AromaX 2030,

Book 03 Brio 2030,

Book 12 The Village 2033-2034,

Book 13 Cologne 2034,

Book 14 Dress for the Ball 2034,

Book 15 Mountain Mansion 2034,

Book 21 Hub 2031,

Book 22 Camp 2034

announce the dangerous presence of AnCors.

The ACA is sounded publicly by the SPs when their sensors pick up the presence of the AnCors. When an ACA alert is in progress, no wheeled vehicles are permitted on the pathways.

This is to allow the SPs on horseback to chase the offender.

For the citizens, the only mode of transportation available for use on the streets during an ACA is anything without a wheel.

This includes trains, horses, or any other mode of transportation not normally used on the street. Since the AnCors use older gasoline-powered cars and trucks, the SPs know that if those are on the road, then there are probably AnCors operating those vehicles.

They become an easy target for the SPs

Administrators These are select people in the education field in Courtly City who structure precisely what each teacher will teach. In this story, Administrator Virginia Hamm gives Sarah Paradise instructions

Book 08 The Lab 2031-2032

for her classroom via Sarah's HIB.

Adventure This is the name of the fragrance which Georgia Peach created in collaboration with Longfellow. It is described as having hints of leather, warm espresso, soft breezes. After a while, you'll detect notes of orange blossoms, roses and a dusting of soft powder.

Book 24 Finally 2035

Aerogel Carbon aerogel epoxy polymer composite can act as a shield against hot and cold

Book 08 The Lab 2031-2032

Aftershake This refers to the tremors felt after a large earthquake or Earthshake has occured.

Book 09 Strawberry EarthShake 2032-2033

Aggregated diamond nanorods (ADNRs) are a nanocrystalline form of diamond (nanodiamond or hyperdiamond). A diamond is carbon made with atoms arranged in a crystal formation (Diamond cubic).
Some very strong diamonds can only be scratched by other diamonds or nanocrystalline diamond aggregate. In the story, Dr. Lou Pole Linden reads, "...Kevlar net against the fullerene carbon- hydrogen nano-structures amorphous diamond film until still pliable. Then shape against desired mold."

Book 08 The Lab 2031-2032

Amiiformes This is a type of freshwater ray-finned bowfin fish which has the ability to head to the surface to breathe or gulp air as if they had a lung. Other names given to this fish include: "cottonfish", "swamp bass", "poisson-castor", "speckled cat", "beaverfish", "cypress trout", and "lawyer". The scientific name for the bowfin is Amia calva. After mating, the male guards the nest to protect their young.

Book 03 Brio 2030

AnCor Anti-Corporatists. AnCors have terrorized Courtly City, and the ACA alert was created because of them.

This group has many chapters, but the one located in Courtly City at the time of this writing is led by Percy Snatcher, who relies on his subordinate, Slash, to carry out his orders.

This group started as a protest against the increasing power of corporations, but bit by bit, the members were cut off from societal resources by the very corporations they tried to fight. As a result, those who are members of the AnCors, at the time of this writing, live "off the grid" of the corporate kingdom.

Book 01 Bubble Year 2030,

Book 02 AromaX 2030,

Book 03 Brio 2030,

Book 11 The Lock 2033-2034,

Book 12 The Village 2033-2034,

Book 13 Cologne 2034,

Book 14 Dress for the Ball 2034,

Book 15 Mountain Mansion 2034,,

Book 16 Investigate 2034, ,

Book 17 Stasis 2034,

Book 19 Impact 2034,

Book 22 Camp 2034,

Book 21 Hub 2031,

Book 23 Plan 2034,

They use older technologies of the past, now abandoned by the citizens of the corporate city. They also have learned to survive by selling their mercenary talents to the highest bidder, which, hypocritically, embodies the very spirit of "anything for a profit" which they claim they are trying to combat in formal corporations.

One chapter in Courtly City is headed by Percy Snatcher, who relies on his subordinate, Slash. They survive by selling their mercenary talents to the highest bidder, which, hypocritically, embodies the very spirit of "anything for a profit" which they claim they are trying to combat in formal corporations.

This group has many chapters, but the one located in Courtly City is headed by Percy Snatcher, who relies on his subordinate, Slash. The group started as a protest against the increasing power of corporations, but bit by bit, the members were cut off from societies' resources by the very corporations they tried to fight. As a result, those who are a member of the AnCors at the time of this writing live "off the grid" of the corporate kingdom. They use older technologies of the past, abandoned by the citizens of the corporate city.

They also have learned to survive by selling their mercenary talents to the highest bidder, which, hypocritically, embodies the very spirit of "anything for a profit" which they claim they are trying to combat in formal corporations.

Ironically, some citizens who are opposed to the indiscriminate power of the corporations quietly live in the society with professions such as investigative reporter or school teacher.

They are in a position to really make a change for the better, but they do it by solving mysteries and exposing the truth, not by threatening innocent lives for a price, as the AnCors of Courtly City do.

This group has many sections, but the one located in Courtly City at the time of this writing is managed by Percy Snatcher, who relies on his subordinate, Slash.

The AnCor group started as a protest against the increasing abusive power of corporations, but, bit by bit, the members were cut off from societies' resources by the very corporations they tried to fight.

As a result, those who are members of the AnCors at the time of this writing live "off the grid" of the corporate kingdom. They also lost the original purpose of the group, which was to fight for worker rights. Instead, they became as abusive as the Corporations, feeling the only way to get anything done was with aggressive violence. They never mastered the art of negotiation. As a result, they never improved their circumstances. They simply became more resentful and angry.

They use older technologies of the past, abandoned by the citizens of the corporate city.

They also have learned to survive by selling their mercenary talents to the highest bidder, which, hypocritically, embodies the very spirit of "anything for a profit" which they claim they are trying to combat in formal corporations.

AR Augmented Reality. This is when you can see some of the real world but with an augmented artistic animation, such as a creature, in your real world. AR means you see both the real

Book 23 Plan 2034

world and virtual world together. VR or **Virtual Reality** means you only see the virtual world

Atlantis nightmare: This is a term Bjorn used on Brio to reference the mythological underwater city of Atlantis, which was supposed to have been a paradise. Yet, because of Bjorn's negative experiences, he calls Brio the Atlantis Nightmare.

Book 04 Courtroom 2031

Automatic (Relating to the character Otto Mattick) Something which works by itself with no direct human control. Actions which are automatic are done without conscious thought. .Used around 1812 to mean moving or acting on its own. The term *automatical* was in use since the 1580s. The term *automatous* has been in use since the 1640s.

Book 21 Hub 2031,

Book 24 Finally 2035

It suggests a machine that performs a function according to a predetermined set of coded instructions in an automatic manner. Some say it is a machine designed to mimic human motion.

Avocados: This is a green skinned fruit with a single seed which grows on evergreen

Book 09 Strawberry EarthShake 2032-2033

208

perennial trees, which grow well in USDA hardiness zones 8 or 9 through 11.
- ☐ Kona Sharwill (B),
- ☐ Sir Prize (B),
- ☐ Reed (A),
- ☐ Pinkerton (A),
- ☐ Holiday (A),
- ☐ Haas (A),
- ☐ Daily 11

The Daily 11 can grow fruit up to 5 pounds, but taste is watery. The Daily 11 is also knowns as *Persea americana Mill*. Descended from Queen avocados (Ventura city, California 1941) they may be the largest grown in California.

Avoid, extreme heat and freezing temperatures. Fruit production increases around 50% when an A Type is near a B type tree. "Near" could be defined as planting (A) trees near (B) trees between 30 feet to a couple of miles away from each other. Some can grow up to 35 feet tall, so home gardeners may need to trim their avocado tree regularly to keep it short so the fruit can be reached without using a ladder.

B

Beholden This adjective describes the process of feeling obligated to somebody, or feeling that you must thank them profusely, because they did you a favor.

Book 15 Mountain Mansion 2034

If you do not want to feel obligated to a person, then you do not like to be beholden to that person.

Bonitor: This is a balloon monitoring system whereby the supervisors project their own two-dimensional faces onto the three-dimensional inflated floating balloon, which is able to move around with remote controls. The Bonitor floats along to monitor staff while projecting their images onto the balloon so the boss does not have to physically be in the room, but checks in on staff remotely.

Book 01 Bubble Year 2030,

Book 03 Brio 2030,

Book 04 Courtroom 2031,

Book 22 Camp 2034

This is the floating balloon monitor which is used by Watson to communicate with the residents of Brio. It allows the user to have a physical presence, yet is navigated remotely so that the user driving the ***bonitor*** can float above the heads of others, which is done in some cultures to establish dominance. This is the monitor where Zor's boss, Watson's face, is projected on the surface of the balloon as it floats around.

The balloon has a camera device where Watson can see what the balloon sees. This is a surveillance tool used by Watson to project his image onto a floating balloon so he can rule by proxy in Brio. He can observe trials and how Zor manages a courtroom.

Botanical. this is a term meaning something which is related to plants. It could be a drug substance made from part of a plant, as from roots, leaves, bark, or berries. In the 1650s, it meant "concerned with the study or cultivation of plants."

Book 02 AromaX 2030

Botticelli. Is the surname of Italian artist Sandro Botticelli who painted in the 1400s in Florence, Italy. He made many famous paintings, including one "Birth of Venus" (1483-1485) which shows a fully grown goddess named Venus arriving on the waves toward shore in an open sea shell to celebrate her birth.

Book 02 AromaX 2030

Brio-crats: This is a term used

Book 04 Courtroom 2031

for the bureaucrats who are in Brio, thinking they are persecuted, whining and bemoaning their plight, when in fact, they are the bullies, whose actions cause confusion and delays to ferreting out the truth.

Burst This is technology that Warren Piece and Longfellow discuss on the Island. Book 05 Chaos 2030-2031

C

Casanova A Fictional character with a reputation for influencing and charming women. Book 06 Dolphin Express 2031

Cassock. Since the 1540s, this term meant a "long loose gown or outer cloak." Book 02 AromaX 2030

Cavalierly is a way to describe a person (adverb) who acts in a manner which indicates they simply do not care about something which should be treated as important. They do not care about the feelings of other people. Book 17 Stasis 2034

Charmeuse This may be from the French word for female charmer, but in this story it references a woven fabric made of silk. The satin weave is made by warp threads crossing over four or more of the backing (weft) Book 24 Finally 2035 threads. This gives one side a smooth shiny finish, while the reverse side has a dull finish.

Cherish. Used since early 14th century meaning to protect and care for someone lovingly.

Book 02 AromaX 2030

Citrus tree varieties: Golden nugget, Pink Eureka lemon, Tahitian lime.

Book 09 Strawberry EarthShake 2032-2033

Cluster. A bundle or batch of something bunched very close together. Around 1727 this was used to define a collection of stars in the sky. Probably from the Old English *clyster* "a number of things growing naturally together".

Book 20 Key Tracks 2034

Clutch A small bag with neither a strap nor handle so that the users must clutch the bag in their hand.

Book 21 Hub 2031

Frequently the clutch carries personal items for a formal evening. The bag usually is small enough to place on a dining table next to the owner. Often this style of bag is ornate so that it looks decorative.

Cologne The fragrance we know today as "cologne", used to reference fragrance from the city of Cologne in Germany.

Book 13 Cologne 2034

Giovanni Maria Farina started developing fragrances around 1709 and may have inspired 4711, which launched in 1792.

Both *Eau de Colognes* contained a blend of Lemon, Bergamot, Orange Oil, Basil and Peach. Middle notes are Jasmine, Lily, Bulgarian Rose, Cyclamen and Melon. Base notes are Oakmoss, Tahitian Vetiver, Cedar, Patchouli, Musk, Petitgrain (orange leaf) and Sandalwood.

This *Kölnisch Wasser* (cologne water) became popular as it was available to the public.

Prior to that, the wealthy had personal perfume creators such as Rene the Florentine who was Catherine de' Medici's personal perfumer. .

Comm This is the device used by residents in Courtly City to communicate on the Courtly network.

Book 06 Dolphin Express 2031

It acts as a cellular telephone. The word was truncated from "communication".

Conundra is the plural of *Conundrom*.

Chapter 30- describing the back cover image on Book 4.

This term means a confusing and difficult problem or question.

Crossbody This is a bag for carrying personal items. Book 21 Hub 2031

It has a strap longer than a shoulder bag because it can be worn across the shoulder or across the torso such that the bag itself rests on the wearer's hip or lower.

Cufflink This is a small object, frequently decorated to be admired. If the cuff has no buttons and only has two small slits, a cufflink connects those two openings on either end of the cuff and secures the cuff around the wearer's wrist. A cufflink acts as a removable button. It is often associated with a more formal shirt. Book 21 Hub 2031

Dance-bot This is a person-sized android or robot which is trained to act as a dance partner. In this story, the dance-bot is wearing a long full skirt to give a male partner training with not only dancing, but also with how to interact with and navigate a human partner's full billowing clothing while on the dance floor. Book 14 Dress for the Ball 2034

<u>EXCERPT</u>

....Bjorn Esterday in white tie and

black coat tails. With him, also in formal attire, was the Dance-bot android. Both spun around the floor with the greatest of ease, causing the chiffon curtains to billow up as they passed

D

Debutant This term was used around 1824 to mean a male performer making his first public appearance.

Book 14 Dress for the Ball 2034

It is from the French *débuter* which translates "to make the first strike" as in billiards. The word "debut" also comes form this word, meaning the first time presented to the public. .

Debutante This term was introduced around 1801. It means a female stage actress making her first public appearance.

Book 14 Dress for the Ball 2034

By 1817, this term was also used to mean a young woman making her first appearance in society. Often her presentation would require a formal ball.

In some cultures, it is customary to wear a long white formal dress and be accompanied by a gentleman wearing formal attire (tail coat).

Demeaned. Caused severe loss of dignity or respect for someone or something else. In use since the 1600's.

Book 02 AromaX 2030

Diplomatic (Relating to the character Diplo Mattick, who was also known as Pat Seeds when in Brio) A way of causing good relations and avoiding bad feelings between parties. Modern meaning could be described as tactful, polite and skilled in win-win negotiations.

Book 24 Finally 2035

Diplomacy is used for aligning governments of different countries. Around 1711 this term was used to relate to official documents and is thought to be from the Latin term *diplomaticus*. There was a collection of important public papers, some of which addressed international affairs. This collection of papers was called the *Codex Juris Gentium Diplomaticus* (1695)

E

Earthie This is a derogatory term referring to a member of the Earth-Farmer Community. The Earth-Farmers, as of this writing, are a group of people who eschew the technology of the modern world in Courtly City and instead quietly and peacefully live and hone farming and other hand-craft skills, including but not limited to quilting. They are considered a Christian religious community which eschews technology. This is a derogatory term which refers to a member of the Earth-Farmer Community. The Earth Farmers are a group of people who eschew the technology of the modern world in Courtly City and, instead, live quietly and peacefully honing farming and other hand-craft skills, including but not limited to quilting.

Book 01 Bubble Year 2030,

Book 02 AromaX 2030,

Book 03 Brio 2030,

Book 12 The Village 2033-2034,

Book 14 Dress for the Ball 2034,

Book 22 Camp 2034

EAMCBS electromagnetic audio mass communication broadcast system. This is used by the SPs to announce the ACA to the people

Book 03 Brio 2030,

EarthShake An archaic translation would be 'earthquake'. .This is a term referring to a shaking of the ground at times, to the point of opening a fissure. Earth tremors occurring after an EarthShake are called an AfterShakes

Earthquakes are measured using scales.

The force, strength and power of an earthquake is measured on the Richter magnitude scale. This measurement of magnitude scale was developed by American seismologist and physicist , Charles Francis Richter, and presented in his paper published with German born Beno Gutenberg in 1935. Later this scale was replaced in 1979 with the moment magnitude scale, which quantified the size of an earthquake. The moment magnitude was inspired by Japanese born Professor Kiyoo Wadati (和達 清夫). Kiyoo Wadati's 1928 paper discussed shallow and deep earthquakes.

This is an example of international science collaboration. One scientific observation supports the development of another. This results in a development which benefit all countries.

Below is a partial list of American earthquakes between 1812 and 1927.

What world events took place at the same time as these earthquakes? What other natural disasters happened? How do you think the people of that time felt?

- ✓ In 1927, Lompoc, CA had a 7.1 .
- ✓ In 1925, Santa Barbara, CA had a 6.8
- ✓ In 1923, North San Jacinto faul had a 6.3 and Humbolt, CA. had a 6.9 earthquake.
- ✓ In 1918, San Jacinto, CA 6.8
- ✓ In 1915, there were two back-to-back earthquakes in Imperial Valley. One registered 6.1 and the other was 6.3.
- ✓ In 1910, Elsinore, had a 6.0
- ✓ In 1906 on April 18th, San Francisco had a 7.9 earthquake. It caused a lot of damage because it struck a populated area.
- ✓ In 1892, Laguna Salada, had a 7.0.
- ✓ In 1872, Owens Valley had a 7.4.
- ✓ In 1857, Fort Tejon had a 7.9 .
- ✓ In 1812, Santa Barbara Channel had a 7.2 earthquake
- ✓ In 1812, San Juan Capistrano, which used to be known as Wrightwood, had a 7.5 earthquake probably on the San Andreas Fault.

Echo In this story, this was a device which would present one location with the holographic live stream image of those in another location. When used with dancing, some refer to the effect as "ghost dancing".

Book 14 Dress for the Ball 2034

EXCERPT
One guest, already inebriated, asked loudly, "When do we get to dance with the Echo?" to which one of the attendants replied, "After the main show, we will signal when you can get back onto the dance floor and ghost dance with Vienna."

Embrace the Erase. This is a phrase used by Watson, the motivational speaker. It was a promise that you could erase everything bad from your past and reinvent yourself with no bad consequences. He used this to sell an imaginary better future.

Book 01 Bubble 2030

Embezzle means to steal funds.

Book 18 Realize 2034

Epinephrine can be another term used for another term for **adrenaline**. It is a hormone and neurotransmitter produced by the adrenal glands. Epinephrine has been used as a drug.

Book 24 Finally 2035

Evermore This is a term used by Longfellow when talking to Bjorn about selecting a mate you can spend your life with. Somebody to trust and respect and love. Book 10 Narci 2033

eVTOL electric Vertical Take Off & Landing vehicle, which is a form of transportation which lands in a Vertiport. Heliports are used for helicopters. Airports are used for airplanes. These "air taxi" can be used for public transportation, but may also require standards for air traffic control. Book 21 Hub 2031

Exocarp In the story, Sarah talks about the outer skin of a tomato. An *exocarp* is the outer layer of the *pericarp* (the outer fruit wall) of a fruit. The middle of the inner skin is called the *mesocarp*, which makes up most of the fruit wall. The inside of the fruit is called the *endocarp*. Book 12 Village 2033-2034

There are many additional parts of the tomato.

In 1965, the Ohio General Assembly made tomato juice the official beverage of Ohio. Since 1870, Ohio has grown tomatoes commercially.

Ohio's Annual Tomato Festival

celebrates the impact of the tomato on Ohio's economy.

Four places with a state tomato are Tennessee, Arkansas, Ohio, and New Jersey.

Exoskeleton In humans, skeletons are the structure which supports the soft tissue in our bodies. In zoology, it means an external hard structure like a shell or armor made of a bone-substance. It became a medical term around 1841.

Book 14 Dress for the Ball 2034

G

Gigapascals, A unit of pressure equal to 10^9 pascals. Geophysicists use the gigapascal (GPa) in measuring or calculating tectonic stresses and pressures. A unit of pressure can quantify internal pressure, stress, and ultimate tensile strength. Aggregated diamonds have an isothermal bulk modulus of 491 gigapascals, which is stronger than carbon diamonds

Book 08 The Lab 2031-2032

Glass Courtroom or **"Glass Court"** This is a term used in Brio to note that the court-case is intended to be as dramatic as possible to provide entertainment

Book 04 Courtroom 2031

to the jury and all those outside the glass wall looking in.

The term indicates that the lives of the residents of Brio are so devoid of mental stimulation that they derive entertainment and experiences which are so extreme it would awaken their senses and make them "feel alive".

In this story, the example is the trial of Bjorn Esterday, who has been burdened by being forced to assume the identity of Otto Mattick.

The jury and onlookers do not know if Otto Mattick is guilty or innocent of the murder of Charlie Horse, but the trial is absurd and not intended to discover the truth.

This is not a genuine court-trial. It is a mere imitation or a glass obscured version of a real trial.

In this story we do not know if Charlie Horse was killed to provide entertainment to the people or not. It is possible Charlie Horse was eliminated because Charlie was a threat to Watson. Did Charlie Horse unearth information which would jeopardize Watson's status and position? Did Charlie Horse seek vengeance because a loved one was conned by Watson?

The whole purpose of the trial is to provide entertainments to the onlookers and possibly be an excuse for Zor, Watson, or any other person in power to quietly get rid of the people they do not like.

This is not a trial of justice. This is not an exercise to find out who is guilty or innocent. Watson's goal is to make this dramatized "trial" as engaging as possible so that many people will watch it from outside the glass wall.

What matters is the show and number of interested viewers. Not the truth. Not justice. Not if anybody innocent gets hurt. Not even if the wrong man gets convicted.

The assumption is anybody outside Brio is fair game and can be slaughtered as nobody inside the group could ever be blamed for wrongdoing....even if they actually were guilty. In Brio, the collective group would deny it to others and even to themselves.

Glek This is a word to describe glamorous items which also use advanced technology. "Glamour" and "high technology" and "fashion" then became "glam-tech", which later became "Glek". Glek is used when referring to glamour technology. Glek fabric was manufactured in AromaX.

Book 08 Strawberry EarthShake

Book 14 Dress for the Ball 2034,

Book 21 Hub 2031

Gloated. This has been used since the mid 1500s to refer to an attentive scornful gaze. A modern definition would be to look at something with smug satisfaction.

Book 02 AromaX 2030

***Glutathione**, antioxidant found in most cells, can prevent damage to important cellular components caused by reactive oxygen species such as free radicals, peroxides, lipid peroxides, and heavy metals*

Book 24 Finally 2035

Grapefruit:
Oro Blanco grapefruit is mentioned in this story, but may have a bitter aftertaste. *Cocktail* grapefruit has a better flavor and is a popular home-garden variety.

Book 09 Strawberry EarthShake 2032-2033

H

Handbag A handbag is something generally carried by a

Book 21 Hub 2031

person to hold personal belongings and money. Some use the term "purse", however, in certain cultures.

A **purse** contains only money and is smaller than a bag held by the hand.

A **pocketbook** was a term used primarily on the East Coast of the United States and refers to a medium sized bag - a bag bigger than a purse, and smaller than a handbag.

A **Shoulder** bag has a strap to wear over the shoulder. A **Cross-Body** bag has a longer strap to wear across the torso. A **Clutch** or **Evening Bag** usually does not have a strap as it is to be clutched in the hand and used for more formal situations.

A **Pannier** bag, or **bike-bag**, references a bag which has two parts to sling over a bike (or horse). It is taken from an old fashioned ladies' undergarment which, in the past, padded out the hips under a skirt. There are many bag types.

Handbag Larger than a purse, this bag carries personal items in addition to carrying currency.

Headquarters This is the location where Longfellow and Warren Piece train the former AromaX recruits on the island.

Book 07 Rough-N-Ready 2031

HIB Holographic Identification Badge. In Courtly City, the HIB uses your profession and then your name instead of a Mr. or a Mrs. so the title would be Teacher Sarah Paradise, Reporter Bjorn Esterday, Administrator Virginia Hamm. The HIB can contain your train ticket. The HIB also conveys instructions for your job, as Miss Hamm gave Miss Paradise her lesson plan instructions.

Book 01 Bubble Year 2030,

Book 08 The Lab 2031-2032,

Book 13 Cologne 2034

HTTYM This is an acronym for a book titled *"How to Troubleshoot Your Mate"*, a book created as if it were a software troubleshooting manual to smooth out problems with your romantic other half.

Book 06 Dolphin Express 2031

i

Idiophone: This is an instrument comprised of parts which make sounds by resonating solid materials.

Book 22 Camp 2034

It is an instrument the whole of which vibrates to produce a sound when struck, shaken, or scraped, such as a bell, gong, rattle, or music box. It produces a sound without any strings. It makes sound by vibrating itself.

Impetuously this is to act suddenly without thinking it through to see if the action is a good idea or not. Example: *Impetuously, she stepped onto the dancefloor.*

Book 15 Mountain Mansion 2034

ImpMi This is a product sold by Watson as a way to escape reality forever. ImpMi is for "improve me". Watson wanted a product name which was easy for the masses to say. In Italian, the word for "me" is sometimes "mi". the phrase *excuse me!* is translated to *"mi scusi!"*

Book 03 Brio 2030,

Book 19 Impact 2034,

Book 22 Camp 2034

In Italian, the words "improve me" could be translated as *migliorami*. Other Italian words to use for the word "improve" could be translated as *ottimizzare, migliorare, perfezionare, progredire, affinare, perfezionarsi,* and more

ImpMis: is the plural of one ImpMi. These were a android-like machine which appeared to be a human being. This was a three-dimensional "avatar" in real life. Watson sold many ImpMis to his followers as a way for them to

229

escape their current life and actually live in a new life of their creation.

Allowing them to escape into a fantasy world, but never allowing them to escape into the real world. Thus the fantasy actually trapped them and caused more problems than if the person had just dealt with their problems in real life.
This product also opened the door for Watson to take their funds while they were distracted by living in an immersive fantasy. His target customers were worried, anxious, lonely people who felt trapped by their circumstances and wanted out. The ideal candidate could be easily angered and made to believe that life was not fair to them and the only way out was with Watson's expensive customized ImpMi device. Using this device prevented those people from building the interpersonal skills to deal with everyday problems.

Watson and Zor would grant this experience to the followers in exchange for access to the end users of this product giving Watson and Zor access to their entire fortunes. This would mean that the person who was the primary source of income could leave and abandon their family and not allow the family to access their own credits, or money.

A one-time payment to "try it out" would be modified by Watson or Zor into a recurring payment until their funds were depleted. Once depleted, there was no need to keep the follower alive.

A temporary stay in a new world, like Brio, would be initially offered as a temporary "try it out" but then extended without the consent of the customer or end-user.

When funds had dried up, those lives no longer mattered and could be discarded with a cover story which claimed the person was doing so well they decided to remain and not take any family nor fiends as visitors.

In reality, those people may have died and been discarded as a cost of doing business. They could have also been sold by the AnCors into slavery in other Corporate cities. Watson had the full support of the Twins.

ImpMi is a Watson product which, when sold, allows Watson to connect to his clients' bank accounts so the customers can be transported to the new ImpMi, which is supposed to make all their dreams come true.

Inclination A desire or leaning towards doing something. Used in the late 1300's (14th Century). From the word *inclinacioun*, which means a condition of being mentally disposed to do something.

Book 20 Key Tracks 2034

Inconsequential This adjective has been in use since the 1620s. At that time, it was used to indicate something was characterized by *inconsequence*.

Book 14 Dress for the Ball 2034

By 1782 it was used to mean something which was not worth noticing.

EXCERPT
This **inconsequential**, humble, little mud-brick hut was, to Male2, the most beautiful home he could imagine.

ipsa scientia *potestas* est This is a Latin term used by Mrs. Libris, the Librarian. The phrase was penned by Francis Bacon in 1597.

Book 01 Bubble Year 2030,

Book 03 Brio 2030,

Book 23 Plan 2034

Some translate it to mean "*Knowledge itself is power*", which Mrs. Libris applies by

232

encouraging the children from Miss Paradise's class to become powerful, honest, honorable citizens armed with factual truth. "ipsa scientia potestas est" "Knowledge itself is power" by Francis Bacon in 1597.

K

Kinematic Relating to the character Kinem Mattick who later was nicknamed Queenie.

Book 21 Hub 2031,
Book 24 Finally 2035

Kinematic is also the study of engineering mechanics focusing on the motion of an object without any reference to the forces which may trigger the motion.

The branch of mechanics focuses on how an object moves and not why it is moving in the first place.

Used around 1840 to mean the "science of motion".

The term ***Cinematic*** was

considered a variant of Kinematic and first used around 1883, but cinematic later became an adjective meaning pertaining to moving pictures or the cinema around 1914.

Laudate Dominium was composed by Wolfgang Amadeus Mozart in Salzburg around 1780.

Book 24 Finally 2035

It was also in *'Silversmith's Pearls of Wisdom'*, which was started in 1776 in the Firebrand series.

The English translation of the Latin is "Praise the Lord all nations; Praise Him all people."

Here are the lyrics to the song in both Latin and in English.

Latin-Laudate Dominium

Laudate Dominum omnes gentes
Laudate eum, omnes populi
Quoniam confirmata est
Super nos misericordia eius,
Et veritas Domini manet in aeternum. Gloria Patri et Filio et Spiritui Sancto.
Sicut erat in principio, et nunc, et semper.
Et in saecula saeculorum.

Amen.

English-Praise the Lord

Praise the Lord, all nations;
Praise Him, all people.
For He has bestowed
His mercy upon us,
And the truth of the Lord endures forever.
Glory to the Father and to the Son and to the Holy Spirit,
as it was in the beginning, is now, and forever,
and for generations of generations.

Amen.

Lexan A transparent plastic (polycarbonate) of high impact strength, used for windscreens in airplane or jet cockpit canopies, bulletproof screens, etc. It is clear enough to see out of like a window, but also very strong.

Book 08 The Lab 2031-2032

Libation Station --Hydration Station These are terms used in Courtly City and AromaX and other Corporate kingdoms to mean a location where one could drink a beverage and relax with friends. .

Book 14 Dress for the Ball 2034

Lipizzaner Became popular around 1928. This term describes a breed of energetic horses developed from Spanish, Italian, Danish, and Arab stock.

When born, they have a dark coat. When they grow up, the coat can lighten to a white color.

The breed started around 1580 when Archduke Charles started a horse stud farm in Lipizza near the Adriatic Sea in modern day Slovenia.

He used the Spanish horses his brother, Maximillian II, imported into Austria. The breed is known to be elegant, strong and beautiful.

Their slightly convex Roman nose gives the horse a distinctive profile. Their white coat is iconic.

These horses were associated with disciplined nobles who refined the art of horseback riding.

Book 15 Mountain Mansion 2034

M

MagSol This is the term used for the enhanced human Dr. Lou Pole Linden's laboratory hoped to produce. This would be a "magnificent soldier" or "MagSol".

Book 07 Rough-N-Ready 2031, Book 14 Dress for the Ball 2034, Book 22 Camp 2034

EXCERPT
...."MagSol", as Linden termed it, describes magnificent soldiers willing to blindly serve the Twins to the death. No questions asked.

The **Magnificent Soldiers** were to be enhanced humans. This project was funded by the Twins who had grabbed power in AromaX.

These MagSols were needed by the twins to seize power in other corporate cities. This is a concatenation of the words 'magnificent soldiers'.

These militarized 'Magsols' are used by the authoritarian Twins to conquer other corporate cities, uniting them under brutal iron rule.

Mailable Inspector Collector

This term is the title of an invention patented in 2021 at the USPTO or United States Patent and Trademark Office. Patent number 11,077,436.

It was created in response to the COVID19 pandemic. This invention was "fast tracked" because it was one of a limited number of patent applications which proved it would benefit the general public and meet other regulatory requirements.

The invention's purpose was to support early pathogen detection (virus or bacteria) in geographies which did not have access to sophisticated laboratory equipment.

The design examined bio-degradable easy-to-access stock supplies to make manufacturing easy. The design also included a process of mass-distribution and recycling for environmentally friendly disposal

It leveraged existing infrastructure for delivery, such as the United States Postal Service or other such courier services. This supply-chain process was included in the design to minimize pollution, trash, litter, and other waste.

When manufactured commercially, it might be referenced with a different name.

Mayfounder Foundation This is a favorite company of Skipper Courtly, the current ruler of Courtly City and the brother of Jack Courtly. It is unclear what this Foundation does, but Skipper says he supports "research. Jack, however. does not like the company. This is explained in the book series EDGES.

Book 01 Bubble Year 2030

Militarized: This term came into use around 1829. It means to convert something into an object used by the military, such as weapons. It could also refer to civilians converted into soldiers.

Book 19 Impact 2034

Misappropriate Means funds which were set aside to be used for one purpose have been misused and applied for a totally different and dishonest purpose. This is usually an unfair action. It could be money intended for an entire group of people yet instead taken and used for one single person. This is a term used to apply to something belonging to another person and is frequently associated with money or funds.

Book 18 Realize 2034

Murse This is a colloquial term coined to mean a purse made specifically for use by a man.

Book 21 Hub 2031

Myoelectric This term means something which relates to electrical impulses generated by the body's muscles. These impulses may be amplified and used for the control of artificial limbs. "Proportional myoelectric control" can trigger robotic artificial limb exoskeletons.

Book 23 Plan 2034

N

NanoNevel This is a technique used in the operating room by training nano-sized (extra tiny) robots to execute a medical surgical procedure at the cellular level. To an observer, this would look like a fog descending on a prone patient and executing the procedure.

Book 08 The Lab 2031-2032, (in the Did You Know section)

Book 14 Dress for the Ball 2034,

Book 17 Stasis 2034,

Book 22 Camp 2034

EXCERPT

...procedure was a surgical technique, which did not require any cuts. The nano-bots had permeated his epithelial tissue with a fog of miniscule robots, whose job it was to attach artificial muscular cells to his own skeletal structure and muscular tissue, making him capable of super-human feats.

The term is used in this story to

define the fog or haze (borrowed from the Dutch language) of nanotechnology which is used during an operation.

NanoNevel manipulates small molecular sized elements infused with artificial intelligence to act as a fog or haze which will descend on a patient and knead or pummel his skeletal structure electrochemically with these nano-structures to interlace the patients own natural muscle fibers with artificial muscle fibers. The collective set of nano bots can be steered or navigated or directed with a program.

These are nano-composite artificial fibers which can lift about 1,000 times or more than regular muscle fibers which had not been enhanced.

A medical procedure used by Dr. Linden in the GONE series to mean nano-sized robots to penetrate the cells, and execute instructions to modify the body on a molecular level. It is conducting an operation without cutting open the patient.

This was a term used to describe a fog of nano-bots which could operate on a living being at the cellular level without making any cuts during the surgical operation.

Narci This word is used to describe a narcissistic personality type. Narcissism is a disorder whereby the person believes they are better than they truly are in reality.

Book 10 Narci 2033,

Book 13 Cologne 2034

They have an over-inflated view of their own self-importance and use self-serving manipulations when interacting with others. In the story GONE, Bjorn is warned to avoid this sort of personality because such characters can not be a romantic dependable partner .

EXCERPT
"Men who describe themselves as a jilted unappreciated nice guy are often not seeing how boorish their manners are. These fellows play victim to the 'nice' stigma.
 ...However, a self-described 'nice guy', [could be] ... rude, insulting, vulgar, unpolished, selfish, and dismissive.
 "...In reality, the True Nice Guy always gets the Evermore woman. Because such gentlemen are charming? Not really. Charm is simply showing another person that you care about them.
 "...That is why you must listen and make an effort to show

your woman you appreciate her."

EXCERPT
"Watson...and Zor...They are both Narcis because all their actions are aimed at controlling their audience..."

So, *Narci* [or *RC*] is just the short term for a person who displays a Narcissistic personality

Negotiation Negotiations take place when two parties discuss a topic designed to result in a final conclusion. This word was used in the 1400's to explain the concept of dealing with people, or trafficking goods.

Book 11 The Lock 2033-2034

It originated from the Old French *negociacion,* meaning "business, trade," and directly from Latin *negotiationem* (nominative *negotiatio*) "business, traffic". Using the term to mean bargaining about anything or a mutual discussion of terms, transactions, or some agreement between two parties actually started around the 1570's.

When negotiating, to see if the other party is in a Bad or Good frame of mind. You may need to mirror their mind-set or be neutral to draw them to a good mood. Some negotiation may be referenced as:

Win-Win: Let's see how we can both get what we want.

Zero-Sum: One of us needs to lose in order for the other to be the winner. I will never trust you. I can only win and take everything if you lose everything. Very competitive.

Stonewalling: I will obstruct your efforts so you cannot get what you want. It doesn't matter if I get anything or not. I want to raise petty objections to make sure you never get what you want. (Used in politics since 1914)

Here is a list of characteristics or attitudes you can observe in the other party to determine if the negotiation is going well (good), poorly (bad) or neutrally (neutral).

BAD
Anger/ Combative
Critical/ Contempt
Sad
Disappoint
Fear
Tension
Stonewalling

NEUTRAL
Not responsive
Expressionless
Shrugging
Steady breathing
Direct stare
Calm
Relaxed body posture

GOOD
Empathy
Compliments/ Validation
Excited
Interest
Smiles
Laughter
Joyful clapping

Neuromuscular electrical stimulation involves sending tiny electrical pulses through the body to cause the muscles to react.

Book 17 Stasis 2034

Noetically- from the word noetic, meaning, "of" or "related to", the mind. Apprehended by the reason or intellect.

Book 24 Finally 2035

Deliberately logical, or an action performed consciously with logic. Thought to come from the Greek *noētikos* (meaning "intelligent") or from *noēsis* (meaning perception, or intelligence, thought).

O

Onsie Usually a garment worn by a toddler to include a single unit of clothing which covers legs, arms and torso and, often, feet.

Book 08 The Lab 2031-2032

OSI Ocular Solar Inhibitor glasses. These may be called "sunglasses". Ocular Solar Inhibitors may be called "anti-sunglasses" by some. or a protective and sometimes polarized eye covering to reduce the glare caused from sunshine.

Book 14 Dress for the Ball 2034, Book 16 Investigate 2034, Book 13 Cologne 2034

Overflow Barn Groomsman The Groomsman is the person to takes care of the horses.

Book 01 Bubble Year 2030

The overflow barn is the place in Courtly City where wild or abandoned horses are rounded up and then later sold to buyers who will own the horses and care for them in their own stables.

Since the ACA, or the Anti Corporate Activity alert, informs the citizens of Courtly City that the AnCor threat is nearby and all wheeled vehicles must cease operations, a horse is needed as a back up mode of transportation.

Using a horse...or a hot-air balloon...are the acceptable modes of transportation citizens can use during an ACA.

P

Paperweight This is a small, heavy object used to hold down loose papers and was first used in 1832. Slang may use this to reference a useless piece of equipment which should be functional but is not and is "just a paperweight".

Book 11 The Lock 2033-2034

Perfusate is a fluid used in perfusion. **Perfusion** describes the process of delivering something via the circulatory system or the lymphatic system to, for example, deliver oxygen or nutrients via blood to an organ or tissue.

Book 24 Finally 2035

Pocketbook A small bag for personal items which is small enough to act as a pocket when the wearer's outfit does not provide pockets. .

Book 21 Hub 2031

Portal chute This is the door way which connects an underwater submersible vehicle or other connecting bridge-like contrivances to the main door of

Book 04 Courtroom 2031

Brio.

Prismatic (Relating to the character Pris Mattick) Something which has the form of a prism, showing a spectrum of colored light. It can reference somethings which act together as one.

Different colored light is not visible until a prism reveals all the separate elements which, when joined, form one bright light.

Used around 1709, the meaning "of or pertaining to a prism". The term *prismatical* has been in use since the 1650s.

PSL Personal Security Lead. This was a person, a bodyguard, employed to guard an area or an individual person.

Purse A small bag to carry everyday personal items. Originated from a small bag to carry coins.

Book 24 Finally 2035

Book 15 Mountain Mansion 2034,

Book 16 Investigate 2034,

Book 17 Stasis 2034

Book 21 Hub 2031

249

Q

Quizzical as in a quizzical expression. This is an expression you get when you are thinking about something that is odd, or you question if it is really true. It could be something which puzzles you. It could also be something which you view as comical but out of place in the situation. In this story, it is used to indicate the character is uncertain about a topic and is questioning the facts.

Book 16 Investigate 2034

R

RC This is the short term for "an Narci", which is short for Narcissist. RC when spoken in English, sounds like "narci" when spoken, so was used as a short name for Narcissistic. . The personality uses manipulation and can be both bully and victim to get what they want. .

Book 10 Narci 2033,

Book 13 Cologne 2034

EXCERPT
"...Narci...or RC....and the way you, Bjorn, behave - your inability to listen - attracts RCs. That is why you are frustrated."

Rebar Probably a shortened version of "enforcement" and "bar". This is a steel rod used as a framework in concrete as a component to a building.

Book 21 Hub 2031

It has been used during construction as it gives extra strength to building walls when that building is subjected to the tremors of an earthquake or *EarthShake*. This term was formally defined around 1961.

The term "rebar" was formally defined around 1961. Some have speculated that Julia Morgan, the first California licensed woman architect, commissioned in the 1920-1930's to design a large estate in San Simeon, California, used the concept of rebar in her earthquake-resistant designs.

How is an earthquake measured?

The force, strength and power of an earthquake is measured on the Richter magnitude scale. This measurement of magnitude scale was developed by American seismologist and physicist, Charles Francis Richter, and was presented in his paper published with German born Beno Gutenberg in 1935.

Later, this 1935 scale was replaced in 1979 with the "moment magnitude" scale, which quantified the size of an earthquake. The "moment magnitude" was inspired by Japanese born Professor Kiyoo Wadati (和達 清夫). Kiyoo Wadati's 1928 paper discussed shallow and deep earthquakes.

This is an example of international science collaboration. One scientific observation supports the development of another. This collaboration results in a global benefit.

Below is a partial list of American earthquakes between 1812 and 1927.

What world events took place at the same time as these earthquakes? What other natural disasters happened? How do you think the people of that time felt?

Here is a partial list of California earthquakes with the year, epicenter city, and estimated magnitude of the quake.

- ✓ In 1927, Lompoc, CA had a 7.1 .
- ✓ In 1925, Santa Barbara, CA had a 6.8
- ✓ In 1923, North San Jacinto fault had a 6.3 and Humbolt, CA. had a 6.9
- ✓ In 1918, San Jacinto, CA 6.8
- ✓ In 1915, there were two back-to-back earthquakes in Imperial Valley. One registered 6.1 and the other was 6.3.
- ✓ In 1910, Elsinore, had a 6.0
- ✓ In 1906 on April 18th, San Francisco had a 7.9 earthquake. It caused a lot of damage because it struck a populated area.
- ✓ In 1892, Laguna Salada, had a 7.0 earthquake.
- ✓ In 1872, Owens Valley had a 7.4.
- ✓ In 1857, Fort Tejon had a 7.9 .
- ✓ In 1812, Santa Barbara Channel had a 7.2 earthquake
- ✓ In 1812, San Juan Capistrano, which used to be known as Wrightwood, had a 7.5 earthquake probably on the San Andreas Fault.

Redmail (Deadmail) This is a term for redacted mail received electronically. RED = *Redacted Electronic Document*. Deadmail is a nickname given by those in Courtly City because at times the document is so redacted that there is no readable meaningful content.

Book 03 Brio 2030,

Book 01 Bubble Year 2030,

Book 11 The Lock 2033-2034

Resentful A person filled with resentment or sour feelings of unforgiveness.

Book 20 Key Tracks 2034

This adjective has been in use since about the 1650s.

Revenge This term was common in the late 14th century. It is from an older version of French *revengier* (Modern French *revancher*), which means to get revenge, avenge, or take vengeance.

Book 19 Impact 2034

Rigorous If this applies to a rule, it means the rule is strictly applied and adhered to. If used to describe something (adjective), it means something which is very thorough or accurate and exhaustive. Strict adherence to a process consistently.

Book 21 Hub 2031

Roadblock A barrier on a road or path. Frequently this is set up by an authority to halt traffic so they may examine something specific. It can also be used figuratively to indicate something blocking your path.

Book 21 Hub 2031

"I hit another roadbock when trying to accomplish my goal."

Rough-N-Ready Location where Longfellow needs to remain periodically.

Book 07 Rough-N-Ready 2031

ROV-**R**emotely **O**perated **V**ehicles. In the story these are called Pods.

Book 05 Chaos 2030-2031

S

Sanguinello Oranges (blood oranges) : The citrus variety of sanguinello often has a rose-tinted rind, but the flesh is a mix of red and yellow. Tarocco Blood orange has more flavor than the Moro, but Moro has deeper red meat.

Book 09 Strawberry EarthShake 2032-2033

SERPENT   Book 05 Chaos 2030-2031

The SERPENT Project logged five sightings of healthy oarfish (*Regalecus glesne*) near the northern Gulf of Mexico between 2008 and 2011. The SERPENT project teams up with offshore oil and gas companies to use their **R**emotely **O**perated **V**ehicles (ROV) as well as other scientific organizations.

SERPENT is an acronym for "**S**cientific and **E**nvironmental **RO**V Partnership using **E**xisting i**N**dustrial **T**echnology" (SERPENT). Note the "N" is capitalized in the word "Industrial" because SERPEIT, using the "I" in "Industrial" instead of the "N", would not be as memorable a name.

Shoulderbag This is a bag to carry personal items but with a strap long enough to wear comfortably over a shoulder.   Book 21 Hub 2031

Silversmiths Pearls of Wisdom This is a work created by a character from the 1770's Firebrand Series. Her name is Silversmith. She created the tradition for Jane Hargreaves.   Book 16 Investigate 2034

256

The tradition has that each generation must add a pearl of wisdom and pass it along to a family member. .

Skipper Courtly is the current ruler of Courtly City. His formal title is Director of the Courtly City Corporation.

His younger brother, Jack Courtly, was ruler before Jack and his family had a terrible train accident (described in EDGES).

After Jack and Queenie's train accident, Skipper became ruler of Courtly City.

SP Soldier Police which are the armed enforcement body assigned to each corporate kingdom, such as Courtly. Each corporate kingdom, such as Courtly, has their own version of SPs.

Book 01 Bubble Year 2030

Book 01 Bubble Year 2030,

Book 02 AromaX 2030,

Book 03 Brio 2030, Book 11 The Lock 2033-2034,

Book 12 The Village 2033-2034,

Book 13 Cologne 2034,

Book 14 Dress for the Ball 2034,

Book 15 Mountain Mansion 2034,

Book 16 Investigate 2034,

Book 17 Stasis 2034,

Book 18 Realize 2034,

Spem in Alium This is the Latin title for the musical composition by Thomas Tallis in 1570. It is translated to mean "Hope in Another". In this story, it was sung during the wedding by forty sopranos, altos, tenors, baritones and bass voices in practiced harmony.

Book 19 Impact 2034,

Book 21 Hub 2031,

Book 23 Plan 2034

Book 24 Finally 2035

Stasis is a state in which something does not change or it remains the same

Book 17 Stasis 2034

Survivor's Guilt When somebody experiences 'survivor's guilt', they have undergone a traumatic event where they survived but others did not. They may think those who did not survive should have, and what a tragic twist of fate that their own lesser lives survived when those more deserving did not. This mental anguish might result from the stressful realization that their own actions could not have altered the outcome because the force of destruction was from a power they could not control.

Book 07 Rough-N-Ready 2031

Sycophants: This term is used to describe a person who acts

Book 19 Impact 2034

insincerely with overly obedient flattery toward an important more powerful person to gain some sort of advantage. The word has been in use since the 1530s. It could mean a talebearer, false accuser, or slanderer who wraps their lies and gossip in flattering words.

T

Tarocco This is a variety of blood oranges, so named because the inside of the orange fruit can range from orange with a blush of pink to a deep ruby red. The Tarocco variety is not as deep red and may actually look like a standard Orange, but the flavor is different.

Book 03 Brio 2030

Transparent Alumina (aluminum oxynitride or AION) This is a transparent polycrystalline ceramic material which mixes aluminum, nitrogen, and oxygen so that you can still see through it in the near-ultraviolet, visible, and infrared light regions. This can be strong enough to withstand shots from small caliber weapons.

Book 08 The Lab 2031-2032

Triptych This is a term used for a three-part painting. A literary or musical triptych is a work which consists of three closely related or even contrasting themes or parts.

See: "About the Back Cover" section referencing book 23, 24, and 25 of the GONE series

U

Unorthodox Something not usually done

Book 08 The Lab 2031-2032

V

Vacate To cause to be empty. To give up or relinquish occupancy of a place. Used around 1640s, "to make void, to annul," from Latin *vacatus*.

Book 20 Key Tracks 2034

VB Virtual Butler

Book 13 Cologne 2034

Vengeance: This is a term in use since the 1300's (14th century). It was from the Latin word *vindicare* which can be interpreted to claim the power to punish or avenge as your own.

Book 19 Impact 2034

There is a Bible verse which instructs Christians to avoid repaying evil with an evil act of your own. Leave retribution to God. Do not take the law into your own hands. Instead, leave any act of punishment to God.

King James Bible- Paul to the Romans in Chapter 12:19-21 ...*Vengeance is mine; I will repay, saith the Lord. (20) Therefore if thine enemy hunger, feed him; if he thirst, give him drink: for in so doing thou shalt heap coals of fire on his head. (21) Be not overcome by evil, but overcome evil with good.*

Vigorously. Done in a way that involves physical strength or effort. In use since the 1300's. Thought to come from medieval Latin, *vigere*, meaning "to be lively, flourish, thrive".

Book 02 AromaX 2030

Book 04 Courtroom 2031

Visual Recall devices (VR)- These devices replay back supposedly recorded footage, but it is difficult to tell if these images are genuine and are essentially used as a prop to create a story to be played out in a Glass Courtroom.

In this story, Bjorn proves how a false image was generated to cast doubt into the "evidence" presented via the VR. VR can be used to reference Virtual Reality in some cases.

VR Virtual Reality.   Book 23 Plan 2034

This is when you can not see any of the real world and you can only see the virtual world. All your senses make you believe you are in a different place.

In this story, VR also means *Visual Recall,* which is a device to capture anything which may need to be recalled in the future. If using the VR term in this way, know that AR is augmented reality. This means that you can see the real world but overlaid are virtual elements. With AR you see both the real and virtual world. With VR you see only a virtual world.

W

Wallet A pocket sized flat folding holder of money, plastic cards, and coins. It sometimes holds important papers needed for travels.   Book 21 Hub 2031

Watsonness This is a term used in Brio. It is used as in "Your lofty Watson-ness".   Book 04 Courtroom 2031

This term is created to stroke the ego of the man who holds power by instilling authoritarian fear in his subject Watson. By addressing him in this manner, a submissive and fearful subjects, who know they are disposable, and also acknowledge there is no word which can describe how great this leader is, so they create a word or title out of his own name.

It is generally done with such exaggerated pomp and circumstance that to an outsider it may seem sarcastic, overly dramatic, or over-done, yet the recipient, Watson, for example, demands such adoration and does not care if it is sincere or not.

wrangler a profession which collects horses from the wild and brings them to the barn to be domesticated or trained so they can be sold.

Book 01 Bubble Year 2030

End of Vocabulary
Please write your notes here.

_____
_____
_____
_____
_____
_____
_____

29 ISBN for all Books

An ISBN, or International Standard Book Number, is a unique numeric book identifier which is used to identify a specific book. If a book store or library does not have the book title in stock, they can find where it is available using the ISBN number.

Book Number	ISBN 13	ISBN 10
GONE Book 01 Bubble	978-1-7184-0030-6	1-7184-0030-6
GONE Book 02 AromaX	978-1-7184-0031-3	1-7184-0031-4
GONE Book 03 Brio	978-1-7184-0032-0	1-7184-0032-2
GONE Book 04 Courtroom	978-1-7184-0033-7	1-7184-0033-0
GONE Book 05 Chaos	978-1-7184-0034-4	1-7184-0034-9
GONE Book 06 Dolphin Express	978-1-7184-0035-1	1-7184-0035-7

GONE Book 07 Rough-N-Ready	978-1-7184-0036-8	1-7184-0036-5
GONE Book 08 The Lab	978-1-7184-0037-5	1-7184-0037-3
GONE Book 09 Strawberry EarthShake	978-1-7184-0038-2	1-7184-0038-1
GONE Book 10 Narci	978-1-7184-0039-9	1-7184-0039-X
GONE Book 11 The Lock	978-1-7184-0040-5	1-7184-0040-3
GONE Book 12 The Village	978-1-7184-0041-2	1-7184-0041-1
GONE Book 13 Cologne	978-1-7184-0042-9	1-7184-0042-X
GONE Book 14 Dress for the Ball	978-1-7184-0043-6	1-7184-0043-8

GONE Book 15 Mountain Mansion	978-1-7184-0044-3	1-7184-0044-6
GONE Book 16 Investigate	978-1-7184-0045-0	1-7184-0045-4
GONE Book 17 Stasis	978-1-7184-0046-7	1-7184-0046-2
GONE Book 18 Realize	978-1-7184-0047-4	1-7184-0047-0
GONE Book 19 Impact	978-1-7184-0048-1	1-7184-0048-9
GONE Book 20 Key Tracks	978-1-7184-0049-8	1-7184-0049-7
GONE Book 21 Hub	978-1-7184-0050-4	1-7184-0050-0
GONE Book 22 Camp	978-1-7184-0051-1	1-7184-0051-9
GONE Book 23 Plan	978-1-7184-0052-8	1-7184-0052-7

GONE Book 24 Finally	978-1-7184-0053-5	1-7184-0053-5
GONE Book 25 Longfellow's Journal	978-1-7184-0054-2	1-7184-0054-3
GONE Book 26 Conversation Station	978-1-7184-0055-9	1-7184-0055-1
GONE Bundle Set of 26 books	978-1-7184-0056-6	1-7184-0056-X

ISBN-13 for EDGES

EDGES Book 1-Swift Encounter	978-1-7184-0002-3
EDGES Book 2-Rousing Attack	978-1-7184-0003-0
EDGES Book 3-One Foot Under	978-1-7184-0004-7
EDGES Book 4-Earthshake	978-1-7184-0005-4
EDGES Book 5-Broken String	978-1-7184-0006-1
EDGES Book 6-Key Witness	978-1-7184-0007-8
EDGES Book 7-Who is She?	978-1-7184-0008-5
EDGES Book 8-Vanish	978-1-7184-0009-2
EDGES Book 9-Chase or Die	978-1-7184-0009-2
EDGES Book 10- Conversation Station	978-1-7184-0011-5

ISBN-13 for FIREBRAND

Firebrand Vol 1- Heed Warnings   978-1-7184-0013-9

Firebrand Vol 2- Perseverance   978-1-7184-0014-6

Firebrand Vol 3- Encounters   978-1-7184-0015-3

Firebrand Vol 4- Seeking Truth   978-1-7184-0016-0

Firebrand Vol 5- Anticipation   978-1-7184-0017-7

Firebrand Vol 6- Seek and Find   978-1-7184-0018-4

Firebrand Vol 7- Secrets   978-1-7184-0019-1

Firebrand Vol 8- Outrage   978-1-7184-0020-7

Firebrand Vol 9- Onward   978-1-7184-0021-4

Firebrand Vol 10- Suspicion   978-1-7184-0022-1

Firebrand Vol 11- Wicked Schemes   978-1-7184-0023-8

Firebrand Vol 12- Confrontation   978-1-7184-0024-5

Firebrand Vol 13- Deliverance   978-1-7184-0025-2

Firebrand Vol 14- Wisdom   978-1-7184-0026-9

Firebrand Vol 15- Holidays   978-1-7184-0027-6

Firebrand Vol 16- Conversation Station   978-1-7184-0028-3

30 About The Back Cover Image

The Wynter Sommers team worked closely with the artist, John dePillis, to summarize themes of the book into a puzzle which can be seen when all the backs of the books are placed in order.

Please turn the books over and line them up to see how each back cover forms a component of the puzzle.

This image depicts several elements which are referenced in the series. The images interwoven with the larger picture, are explained in this section. The artist was inspired to adopt the theme of each book and depict the essence of each theme with visual elements.

With each book, please feel free to have an open discussion about the artwork which appears on the back of each book. Ask what that theme means to the reader. Ask what other message reveals itself to the reader and why. Have a group discussion regarding how you relate to the image and what message you get from viewing the individual back cover, as well as the cover as a whole.

A full page version of this image is at the end of this section. The image, without the numbers, is also at the end of this section.

Gone Book 26 Conversation Station--About Back Cover Image

📖 **Book 1**: The image on the back of this book depicts a dove of peace. It is the motivation for many characters. Additionally, it contains an orange blossom as a hint to AromaX, the city where the major export is glamour, cosmetics, and fragrance. In later chapters, the book references the German city of Cologne, where the first bottled fragrance, which uses orange blossoms, was popularized.

The petals are speckled for two reasons.

First, the colors are from the forest-like background to represent how Longfellow hid and took refuge in the forests of a foreign land.

Second, the speckles also represent the taint of corruption which swooped into

270

AromaX and gripped the seat of power, taking over in an authoritarian manner.

Once the Mattick family was ousted from power, AromaX product quality, including fragrance exports, declined. This impacted the economy forcing the educated citizens of AromaX into avenues of poverty.

The speckled orange blossom, one of the most fragrant of flowers, is a reminder that truth and objective justice must prevail to allow for a thriving prosperous economy. The orange blossom also represents the Southern California orange groves near the home of the author.

The theme of this image is:

Misinterpretation. Take time to double check the facts and get the whole story. It is foolish to act on the impulse of fervent emotion. Wait until you get the true interpretation of events and facts.

Book 2: Alludes to an image of the blue sky of freedom mingled with the warm pink-rosy sunset, indicating the end of an era where the wildlife could breathe free. The horse represents the training Longfellow required of the AromaX refugees. Bjorn also had to learn to ride a horse while he was a reporter to respond to the ACA, Anti corporatist alerts. Here, the horse represents an alternate mode of moving forward during difficult times. The pure white mane of the horse represents freedom and purity. The mane becomes part of book 3, where it fades into the forehead, or the thoughts of the image. The horse becomes part of her hair and forms one edge of an eyebrow.

The theme of this image is:

Leadership. Any organization with corrupt leadership will suffer. Selecting a wise moral leader is vital.

Book 3 shows the wisps of the mane at the forehead to indicate that the human face is contemplating the past and wondering how to move into the future. Here you see orange blossoms which are clean and not speckled. This is to symbolize the forging strategy of the future.

The economy of the past, along with the image of the white mane, indicates that a strategy for moving forward is being contemplated. There is more vivid green in this image which shows a progression toward regaining balance, health, and normalcy after an offensive attack.

The theme of this image is:
Destiny. Know what is in your control to manage with discipline and perseverance. Know what elements are out of your control and choose your attitude with optimism tempered by realism.

📖 **Book 4** depicts the muzzle of Tustin, the "toffee-nosed" poodle. Being "toffee nosed" means pretentiously superior or snobbish. Here the poodle represents status and an owner of a poodle may be viewed as more discerning, and appreciating the finer things in life. In the story, however, Tustin is an intelligent active and loyal canine.

The theme of this image is:
Opportunity. Be alert to opportunities concealed by *conundra*. Make the effort to keep moving forward on a nobel path, despite the odds against you. Some progress is better than no progress.

📖 **Book 5** shows the rest of the fluffy white poodle, Tustin, as well as Justin, the Belgium Malinois. Another one of Longfellow's faithful and well trained disciplined canine friends. Notice here, the dog blends into the bark of trees in the background which also forms the hair of a female figure.

The theme of this image is:
Chaos or the loss of predictable structure. When encountering situations which are chaotic, rely on your faithful alliances and create the order needed. You may discover others are glad you offered structure until the chaos subsides.

Book 6 shows the stealthy dog Dustin, the Labrador retriever who is as dark as dust. This breed has been used as a guide for the blind, but is also a faithful companion when hunting. In the image, the dog picks up the dark forest green of Longfellow's refuge in the islands. This dog does help Longfellow see, strategize, and hunt injustice.

The theme of this image is:
Pride. Sometimes we think better of ourselves and appear to be filled with contempt for those "lesser". Know that each individual has a way of adding to the success of a situation, no matter how small the contribution. What is hiding in your personality? Shouldn't your actions be guided by selfless kindness to better the community?

📖 **Book 7** shows the soft hue of pink, a blush on the cheek of a woman. This warm wash of color could be the cloud near a setting sun as well as the soft peach of a woman's cheek. Blushing shows modesty and even embarrassment. Here we now see, the woman's hair, which could also be the trunk of a tree. The forest represents Longfellow's hiding place, and eventually a refuge for Bjorn Esterday. The blush represents a figure who may have been initially tricked into relinquishing power, as was done in AromaX, but also the determination to right the wrongs inflicted on her people.

The theme of this image is:

Goals. "A man's accomplishments in life are the cumulative effect of his attention to detail." This is a quote from John Foster Dulles, American Diplomat (1888-1959). This informs us that we need to select a goal, define the smaller steps to achieve that target. Then, to make an effort to execute the steps while paying attention to the details.

Gone Book 26 Conversation Station--About Back Cover Image

📖 **Book 8** reveals three birds in flight. One with a teal green-blue belly, representing the blue skies of a better future. The green represents tinges of jealousy which infect our motives. From a distance, this bird could also appear to be a eye, which represents how we look at and interpret events. The two playful ravens below form the nostrils of a nose. A group of ravens is known as a conspiracy. The artist chose the raven to indicate that we cannot be swept up by conspiracies and we need to learn to "breathe free". One way to do that is to innovate new solutions to current problems.

The theme of this image is:
Innovation. Some believe that a roadblock forces us to create solutions. Plato once wrote "our need will be the real creator". Some believe this phrase was modified in English to be "Necessity is the mother of invention". The theme of this book is to not be confused by popular interesting conspiracies, which are presented in a way that make you feel elite and as if you are one of the chosen few to understand this obscure insight. Rather, it is to be objective about the facts, to define the true problem, and then innovate a solution.

📖 **Book 9** shows a second bird with a colorful belly forming the woman's second eye. The bird above, which creates an eyebrow, is flying in a different direction. This is to represent that any path could be taken. When making a choice, it is best to deliberate and then fly to your next destination, but give yourself room to course correct, if needed. This is what the characters in this story had to do.

The theme of this image is:

Ingenuity. To innovate, you must be clever and original. To create, you must know in what direction you are headed. The birds flying in opposite directions remind us to focus on developing, and to stay the course.

📖 **Book 10** is the fifth book of the second row. This also shows a horse, which blends into the bark of a tree. The blue sky in the top left of the pane also represents the crisp air, the oxygen needed to be free from narcissistic personalities and to move forward.

The theme of this image is:

Narcissism. How do we avoid grabbing power with narcissistic manipulations? How do we identify harmful anarchistic personalities and be productive?

📖 **Book 11** is the first book on the third row. Here we see a tangle of branches and leaves representing the way a problem can obscure our view. This is a modern depiction of how solutions can be hidden from view when we first look at a problem, focusing on the wrong things. When we look at all the books put together as a whole, we see a different single image emerges pulling all the smaller pictures together. Can you see the forest or the tree? This image reminds us to see the whole picture.

The theme of this image is:
Imposter Syndrome. Sometimes we feel as if we fade into the background, as represented by the mass of branches and leaves. As if the achievement we have accomplished isn't because we are really talented, but that the credit was granted to us through a fluke of events. We must realize we are talented and do deserve the credit for the work we did. We have permission to stand out instead of hiding in the background. We need to remove the clutter of figurative branches to make our path clear.

📖 **Book 12** shows the face of Austin, the plucky Jack Russel Terrier, another dog of Longfellow's canine pack. The dog fur blends into the tree bark. The lines which create the grain in the bark of the tree trunk, also form locks of hair.   Sometimes hidden, Austin symbolizes the ability to blend in, yet pop out with energy when needed.

The theme of this image is:

Home. Familiar surroundings make us feel comfortable and feel "at home." After an absence, when we return home, we welcome an enthusiastic greeting, such as one provided by an energetic Jack Russel Terrier. Here we are reminded of what emotions make us feel we are at home.

📖 **Book 13** is the very center of the entire image. This is the third book of the third row. Here the red bird forms the lips of the woman. Is she ready to speak her mind? Is she guarded about her words? Here we can now reveal that this woman is a composite of Georgia Peach, who may not be what she seems. But Georgia has befriended Sarah Paradise, who also shares the same struggles, making her empathetic with Georgia. In uncertain times, who can you trust?

The theme of this image is:

Legacy. This image is in the very center of the entire larger painting because the words we speak are very important. It is how we leave an impression, which culminates into the legacy we leave behind. The red bird symbolizes bold courageous passions. The bird forms lips to speak the words which support nobel causes.

📖 **Book 14** this book image shows the jaw of the woman. It shows a firm determination, indicating a readiness to plunge forward with grit. The lines forming the tree bark, also comprise locks of hair. This image is part of the image on the back of book 15.

The theme of this image is:

Anticipation. This abstract image conveys the eagerness to move forward tempered by the determination to encounter any difficulties.

📖 **Book 15** The bark of a tree trunk reveals a smiling face embedded in the wood grain. The artist motivation for placing this face here was explained to mean that our spirits and motives reveal themselves in objects around us and even in the work our hands produce. If we are happy, then even the tree nearby will appear happy. If we produce goods with ethics and integrity, then those using our finished goods will reap the benefits. If we wish others to smile around us, we must first smile ourselves and be lavish with sincere compliments and appreciation about even the smallest of things.

The product or service we generate will contain traces of our motives and attitude and our personalized spirits will be apparent in our final product.

Bottom line is, do you believe that what you do matters and has an impact?

background. Could this half hidden image represent longing for a past love, who imparted memories now ingrained into her heart? This may be why he is depicted as part of the wood of the tree bark. The barcode in this image has been placed to cover one eye. The artist did this to indicate that when in love, you have one eye focused on the object of your desire to make sure no harm comes to them.

The theme of this image is:

Fate. Are there coincidences in life, or are repeated circumstances presented before us, to give us the option to seize an opportunity? How did fate treat the love of Longfellow? How does fate play in your life?

Gone Book 26 Conversation Station--About Back Cover Image

📖 **Book 16** is the first book on the fourth row. Here we see the head of a dolphin, which springs up from the waters below to play with a companion dolphin on Book 17. Dolphins were vital for Bjorn's survival.

<u>*The theme of this image is*</u>:

Investigate. In this story, some of the characters are brought to the brink of exhaustion, ready to give up. Then an opportunity is presented. Dolphins are smart and help Bjorn when he thinks there are no other options. We can choose to give up or investigate for even an unlikely solution. This image encourages the reader to investigate options.

📖 **Book 17** shows the second dolphin popping up from the bottom of the image to play with the dolphin on Book 16. Also we see the start of the woman's necklace, a string of figurative pearls which represent the necklace of islands which provided refuge and rest to Longfellow's recruits, and Bjorn. Here the flock of birds cover Book 17 18 and 19. This flock of birds not only form a necklace, but also represent refuge and sanctuary. This is the place you rest and recover while you plan your come-back.

The theme of this image is:
Stasis. When will we set aside time to be still and recover from a trial? Stasis implies that we have stopped moving, We are still and quiet for a time. We need to learn when to be still and recharge. We need to know when to start up again, move, and head to a specific goal.

Book 18 illustrates the throat of the woman. Here, her voice mingles with the bird's song. The background of her neck is a soft cloudy warm evening sunset, depicting dusk. We realize that evening and night will soon be here revealing the bright diamond-like stars carpeting the heavens. Deliberate words have just been spoken and now we realize it is time to stop talking and close our lips and listen. Wait. Results will be revealed in the morning.

The theme of this image is:
Realize. We must realize there is a time and place for all actions and we must discern those situations with wisdom.

📖 **Book 19** This fourth book of the fourth row is also the last part of the woman's flock of birds necklace. Here the image shows us the blanket of leaves in the forest, some of which form the image of a bird. Because the bird is comprised of leaves, it indicates a fleeting message, which we must listen to in order for that message to provide maximum impact. Sometimes the most powerful events approach us silently and in disguise, camouflaged until the right time to convey the message.

<u>The theme of this image is</u>:

Impact. For maximum impact we must exercise restraint, discipline and patience to know just the right time.

📖 **Book 20** shows the fifth book in the fourth row. This contains a portion of the man from Book 15 at the top, and the bird of leaves at the bottom. This picture brings together all the components of patience and lost love. Love can be found, again. This panel represents hope.

<u>The theme of this image is</u>: **On Track**. We know we are on track when our motives reflect a pure-heart, our actions demonstrate practiced expertise, and our words reveal discernment.

📖 **Book 21** is the first book on the fifth row. We see the churning ocean which concealed Zor's Brio. The sea is animated to reflect ever churning change which must be navigated.

<u>The theme of this image is</u>:

Hubs and Connections. When we are at a crossroads, and need to decide which way to move in life. We must ensure we do not get paralyzed or overwhelmed with too many options. If you do not know which way to go, start with which way you do not want to go and eliminate all the bad choices up front. Then, when you are at your figurative hub, only evaluate the good options and then move forward, knowing you can evaluate and change course.

📖 **Book 22** This is the second book of the fifth row. This shows the body of the dolphin jumping out of the churning water as Brio fell. Bjorn belonged in Courtly City, not Brio. Was Brio a refuge or a prison?

<u>The theme of this image is</u>:

Belong. You feel as if you belong in the place you feel accepted. Where do you feel the sense of belonging?

📖 **Book 23, 24 and 25** With these three pictures, we see the image of the whale witnessed by Bjorn when first introduced to Brio's courtroom. The story does not mention the type of whale. Here the artist was inspired as he created this Triptych, or three-panel painting. We see a cloud which resembles the pilot whale. The image reminds us when Bjorn was in an impossible situation, and eventually resolved it. Does the cloud-whale symbolize elusive love?

The artist drew inspiration from the pilot whale for two reasons: First, the social pilot whales remain with their families, or birth pods, for life. Second, this "black fish" has a pale marking on the underbelly which resembles the shape of a heart. This heart-shaped marking supports the subtle romantic element of the Gone series.

The theme of Book 23 is: **Plan.**
The theme of Book 24 is: **Finally**.
The theme of Book 25 is: **Longfellow's Journal**.

The theme of these images reflect the full circle of the story. The saga opens when Bjorn sees the whale. Here the image ends in the lower right with an image of the whale swimming among choppy waters to contrast a calm large whale navigating the turbulent surroundings.

The whale cannot leave the situation, but the whale can dive deeper. Alternatively, to get a fresh perspective, perhaps the whale has surfaced to confront oncoming waves.

Then, again, perhaps the waves about to crash around the whale really are friendly dolphins and are nothing to fear at all. It depends on your perspective and your situation.

This imagery represents how we plan as we strive to meet our goals. Do we move forward even if we feel our contributions are invisible or insignificant? We must boldly embrace the brisk fresh air of our unknown futures.

Every act, no matter how tiny, when laced with integrity, morality, and understanding, will make an impact.

The turbulent seas of life may force us to redefine our final goals and the strategy to obtain that goal. We will be devoted to continual learning and being a better person today than we were yesterday.

One day, we will find satisfaction in finally attaining our goal in a manner which improved the lives of those we encountered along our journey. We need to make life better selflessly for others as we progress along our path.

As you assemble all the back covers, how does the image speak to you? What do you get out of it?

Gone Book 26 Conversation Station--About Back Cover Image

The book numbers are assigned to each segment of the image. Place all the backs of the books together to reveal the image.

288

This is the image without the book numbers

Gone Book 26 Conversation Station--About Back Cover Image

Our goal is to create art with words and images which evoke conversation. Discuss provoking heartfelt topics. What creates longing? What quenches desire? How do you show comfort to another in pain? How do you define a friendship? What is wisdom and discernment? How would an ordinary person behave when foisted reluctantly into extraordinary situations? How would you respond?

To which characters do you relate? How do you demonstrate the value of peace, honor, integrity, truth, patience and perseverance to overcome obstacles in real life. How do you inspire others to be their best? What do you do to bring out the best in others?

Wynter Sommers hopes each tale compels you to become more creative with small kindnesses shown to your neighbor. One never knows when a small choice today will impact generations into the future.

Choose wisely. True love is the most durable substance on earth. Wynter Sommers hopes you enjoy the books in the GONE series, as well as the EDGES and FIREBRAND and DAISY's ADVENTURES series. Explore.

31 ABOUT Wynter Sommers

Wynter Sommers is the pseudonym for an American writing team, which harnesses multiple skills in technology, research, history and education. Formally trained with a PhD in Education, Wynter Sommers blends academic classroom experience, with corporate sophistication, and a passion for developing more effective student insights through engaging storytelling. Wynter Sommers has a heart to inspire creativity and develop critical thinking skills, all to encourage readers to make wise choices in life.

Wynter Sommers takes each story and weaves the plot with classic gripping elements, which endure throughout repeated readings, revealing new meanings each time the story is explored. The small choices a reader makes in real life could have a lasting effect in future generations. This set of stories shows the origin of not just Bjorn Esterday and Sarah Paradise, but of their ancestors and the sort of world which was established, which unfolded in each generation until Bjorn and Sarah met.

It is rewarding to learn of heartfelt, thought provoking conversations taking place globally about the characters of these books. Should the reader be presented with extraordinary circumstances, it is the sincerest wish that they act with honor, truth and integrity to overcome obstacles in real life whilst the reader hones skills of self-reliance and collaborative teamwork despite barriers outside of the reader's control. Wynter Sommers hopes you enjoy the other **Bjorn Esterday Was not Born Yesterday** stories in the EDGES series and GONE series.